S.CREAM SHOP

Eye Spy Aliens

By Tracey West

For my dear friend Alice, who may or may not be from another planet. Thanks for making Earth a better place!—T.W.

To my parents Eileen and Bill, who gave me the love, tools and support to chase my dreams.—B.D.

Library of Congress Cataloging-in-Publication Data is available.

ISBN 0-448-43226-9   A B C D E F G H I J

S.cream Shop

Eye Spy Aliens

By Tracey West

Illustrated by Brian W. Dow

Grosset & Dunlap • New York

"Ouch!"

Evan Kim stomped his painfully tingling right foot on the sidewalk. He had been crouched behind the mailbox for nearly an hour now, and his foot had fallen asleep.

Evan thought about giving up. His friends Billy and Todd were probably home right now, playing video games.

But a good spy never gives up, Evan reminded himself. *Patience is the key to a successful investigation.*

Evan's foot stopped tingling, so he crouched down once more. He held the lens of his mini-periscope up to his eye. The periscope allowed Evan to spy without being seen. A tube rose straight up from the lens and peeked over the top of the mailbox, giving Evan a perfect view of his target: Sebastian Cream's Junk Shop.

He officially became a spy three months ago, when his older sister, Tina, gave him the book *Harriet the Spy* for his twelfth birthday. At first he'd thought it was a dumb present—he liked playing video games much better than reading, and besides, there was a girl on the cover—but Tina made him promise to read at least the first chapter. She said she'd give him a dollar if he decided not to read any more after that.

Evan never got the dollar. He read the whole book in three days. He liked how Harriet followed a route every day and spied on the people in her neighborhood. And he really liked the cool belt she wore, with a flashlight and other spy equipment attached.

So Evan had started saving up his allowance. Instead of buying video games with it, the first thing he bought was a belt, along with a bunch of metal clips he could hang from it. Then he bought a flashlight and a small notebook, just like Harriet used. In the toy store, he found a whole section of Junior Spy Equipment, which worked pretty well even though they were all made from bright red plastic—not very spy-like at all, Evan thought. So far, he had the binoculars, the periscope, and a microphone that amplified sound so he could hear people talking from far away. He was saving up for the night-vision goggles.

Of course, he was pretty sure his parents wouldn't let him go on his spy route at night, but the goggles might come in handy someday. Yet, during the day, he spent about an hour-and-a-half after school on his route, which had changed over the last few weeks.

He had started out by following his mail carrier, but that had become boring pretty quickly. Mrs. Rodriguez never did anything except deliver mail and make dogs bark like crazy. Following the pizza delivery guy from Mario's Pizzeria hadn't been that exciting, either, although it did make Evan pretty hungry.

So Evan had decided on another plan. He would spy on some key buildings in town and see if anything happened there. He spent a week at the First National Bank and was disappointed that he didn't see even one suspicious character scoping the place. He tried the supermarket and the ice-cream parlor, but those just made him hungry again.

But his outings weren't useless. He had started to hear people talking . . . whispering about a strange new shop that had opened downtown. A shop run by a funny little man who sold unusual items.

Then one day he heard a tall, red-haired woman talking to another woman as she left the ice-cream parlor.

"It's called Sebastian Cream's Junk Shop," she said. "You really must go. I've never seen anything like it."

Evan was intrigued. What kind of a name was 'Sebastian Cream,' anyway? It sounded pretty suspicious to him.

And so now Evan found himself crouched

behind a mailbox on Wary Lane as he spied on the junk shop. With his periscope, he had a pretty good view of the store. He could make out most of the items jumbled in the window: an old wooden chest that looked like a treasure chest; stacks of books; a large, faded sign from an old hamburger stand; and a group of china dolls with staring blue eyes.

Through the clutter, Evan could sometimes see a small, round man puttering about the store. He wore wire-rimmed glasses, and a ring of white hair topped his otherwise bald head. Evan guessed this was the mysterious Sebastian Cream.

Other than the shop's owner, Evan hadn't seen anyone enter or leave the store.

That's definitely suspicious, Evan thought. He lowered the periscope and made a note in his notebook.

Store has no customers. How does he stay in business?

"Is there something I can do for you, young man?"

Startled, Evan fell sideways into the mailbox. He dropped his notebook and pen.

Sebastian Cream himself was standing over Evan, peering at him through his glasses. The little man looked much larger from Evan's point of view. He quickly scrambled to his feet.

"Uh, no, I'm fine," Evan said, cringing as the words came out. He didn't sound very spy-like at all.

Mr. Cream eyed the spy equipment on Evan's belt. "I see you collect tools of investigation," he said. "Why don't you come into my store? I think I have the perfect item for you."

Evan hesitated. The strange shop owner obviously suspected Evan was spying on him. Why was he being so friendly?

Evan cast the thought aside. He had come to investigate the junk shop. A good spy wouldn't turn back now.

"Sure," Evan replied. He picked up his notebook and pen, then followed Mr. Cream across the street and into the shop.

The little man went straight to a glass case. He took a key from his pocket, opened the case, and took out what looked like a black tube, about six inches long. He handed the tube to Evan.

Evan saw that the tube had a lens on either end, one slightly bigger than the other. He held the smaller end up to his eye and looked through it at a moose head on the wall. Through the lens, the moose head looked like it was right in Evan's face.

"It's a spyglass," Mr. Cream said, smiling.

"It's pretty cool," Evan admitted. "But I

already have binoculars and a periscope."

Mr. Cream clicked his tongue. "Those are just child's toys. This spyglass is much more special. It's the only one of its kind."

Evan frowned. It looked pretty ordinary to him. He handed the spyglass back to Mr. Cream. "No, thanks," he said.

Mr. Cream looked thoughtful. "I'll tell you what," he said. "Try it out for free for one week. If you don't like it, you can return it—no charge."

Evan considered this. The spyglass wasn't anything special, but it was definitely more professional-looking than his plastic stuff. He wasn't sure what Mr. Cream was up to, but this would definitely be his chance to find out, wouldn't it? Evan nodded. "It's a deal," he said.

"Splendid!" cried the shopkeeper. He walked behind his counter, pulled out a small paper bag, and put the spyglass inside. Then he handed it to Evan. "I'm sure you'll find it quite interesting," he said.

Evan hurried out of the store. On the way out, he bumped into a girl from his school, but he didn't stop to talk. He couldn't wait to get home and write down what had happened in his notebook.

Of course, he wanted to try out the spyglass, too. Evan looked at his watch. It was almost five o'clock. He'd have to finish his homework and then eat dinner. By the time he got to try out the spyglass, it would be dark.

Maybe he was rushing things. He could plan out a new route and try out the spyglass tomorrow afternoon. After all, it was just an ordinary spyglass.

Wasn't it?

If Evan tries out the spyglass that night, go to page 133.

If Evan waits until tomorrow to try out the spyglass, go to page 36.

Continued from page 37

Evan decided to check out the Universal Fruit Outlet. The mayor's box didn't seem all that interesting. It probably just held groceries or mayor-type papers or something.

Evan looked around for a good spying place. A row of leafy, green bushes hedged the sidewalk just across the street. Perfect.

Evan walked behind the bushes, made sure no one was looking, and then crouched down. Sharp branches scratched his face and arms as he moved in, trying to conceal himself among the leaves.

He finally found the perfect spot. A natural break in the bushes allowed him a perfect view of the fruit outlet's front door. Evan reached for his binoculars, then remembered the spyglass. He unclipped it from his belt and held the lens to his right eye.

"Wow," Evan said softly. The spyglass worked great. It seemed like the front door was right in front of his face.

Just then, someone stepped in front of the door. It was an older woman in a red coat. Her curly gray hair stuck out from underneath a silver helmet on her head.

Evan lowered the spyglass and frowned. What was with the helmet? It looked like a bike helmet that had been covered with aluminum foil. Maybe it was some old-lady fashion thing.

Shaking his head, Evan looked through the spyglass again. The old lady entered the building. Then two men walked up and knocked on the door.

They both wore business suits—and silver helmets.

This was definitely getting interesting. Evan reached over to his notebook and scribbled in a quick note about the helmets.

Evan looked through the spyglass again. The two men had entered the building, and now a guy who looked a little older than a teenager was approaching the door. He wore a T-shirt with a flying saucer on it, scruffy jeans, black sneakers with holes in them—and a silver helmet.

The guy stopped and looked around before he went inside, as though he wanted to make sure no one saw him.

Then his gaze stopped on Evan. He let out a big grin.

"Oh, no," Evan groaned. He had been spotted. He pushed his way through the scratchy branches, which kept getting stuck on his belt. By the time he made it out, he found himself face-to-face with the flying saucer T-shirt guy.

"Cool gear, dude," the guy said, still smiling.

"I'm Alex. Are you here for the meeting?"

Evan wasn't sure what to say. He decided to play along. "Uh, sure," he said.

"I thought so," Alex said. "I was pretty nervous before my first meeting, too. I scoped the place for a few days to make sure everything was cool. But you don't have to worry. Everything's cool."

"Cool," Evan echoed. "That's great."

"Well, come on," he said. "We've got to get you a helmet."

Evan hesitated, but just for a second. He had to know what those helmets were all about. He followed Alex across the street into the Universal Fruit Outlet.

Go to page 52.

Continued from page 122

"I guess you're right," Evan told Simon. "But tell me something first. Why were you spying on the mayor? And how do you know he's an alien?"

Simon's smile got wider. "If I told you, I wouldn't be a very good spy, would I?"

Evan knew Simon had a point. "You're right. So what do we do now?"

Simon opened up his denim jacket. All of his spy tools hung from hooks sewn inside the jacket. But they were silver and more professional-looking than Evan's tools. He unhooked a small pair of binoculars and turned toward the mayor's window.

Evan nodded and lifted the spyglass to his eye. Mayor Jones was still scarfing down onions, tearing at their flesh with his sharp alien fangs.

Then the mayor's door opened, and four more aliens wearing business suits came in. When Evan lowered the spyglass, he saw that they all looked like middle-aged men.

Mayor Jones greeted the men. Then he did something strange. He reached up and yanked at his hair, pulling at his face. His human face came off like a mask. Evan could see his alien face without the spyglass now.

The men took off their masks, too, and then they all chowed down on the onions. When there were no onions left, they began to talk.

Evan unclipped his microphone and held it up, but he couldn't hear a thing. "Rats!" he said. "They're too far away."

"Then we will get closer," Simon said.

Evan and Simon walked closer to the back wall of the building. Even though the mayor's office was on the first floor, it was still fifteen feet above the ground. Luckily, some metal garbage cans were nearby. Evan and Simon dragged them over to the window and climbed on top. Evan held his microphone up as far as he could, and the sounds of voices came through.

"We have operatives all over the planet now," one of the aliens was saying.

"Yes," said another. "As soon as we give the word, our invasion can begin."

"Earth will be ours!" said another, and then all of the aliens let out a cheer.

The loud sound blew through the microphone, startling Evan. He fell backwards off of the metal garbage can, which crashed to the ground with a clatter.

"Evan!" Simon cried, jumping down.

Above them, the mayor's window flew open. Mayor Jones stuck his head out of the window, an angry look on his face. "Spies!" he cried. "Capture them!"

The rest of the aliens poured out of the window and started climbing down the wall like they had suction cups for fingers.

Evan and Simon had to run—but where? They could run around the building into the park. Or they could climb the fence behind them, on the other side of the empty lot. They might be able to lose the aliens that way.

If Evan and Simon run to the front of the building, go to page 45.

If Evan and Simon run to the wall behind them, go to page 93.

"Let's hear your idea, Evan," said Betsy. "You were very smart to figure out about the helmets. I'm sure your idea's a good one."

"Well," Evan said, "I think we should take the alien technology out of our helmets and then put them on. When the aliens come, they'll think they're still controlling us. But they won't be, and then maybe we can turn the tables on them."

"Brilliant!" Betsy said. "What do you say, everyone?"

The group agreed it was a good idea. They went back upstairs and retrieved their fallen helmets. Evan quickly showed them how to remove the alien wires. Then they put on their helmets and went back down to the basement.

The final countdown had begun. Everyone watched as the last ten seconds ran down.

10 . . . 9 . . . 8 . . . 7 . . . 6 . . . 5 . . . 4 . . . 3 . . . 2 . . . 1 . . .

As the number 0 flashed, the large crystal began to glow again. An alien materialized inside the dome. But this was no hologram. This one was real. It stepped outside the dome, into the basement.

Right behind it, another alien materialized in the dome. It stepped out next to its partner. The

18

two aliens looked around the room, nodding.

"Excellent," said the first alien. "These humans did an excellent job building our transporter for us. Now they are our willing slaves."

"Agreed," said the second alien. "What task shall we give them?"

"Have them guard the crystal," said the first. "If anything happens to the crystal, we won't be able to remain on this planet."

"Why not?" asked the other.

"Weren't you paying attention in invasion class?" snapped the first. "The crystal is creating an energy field that sustains our existence here. Without it, we'll be transported back to Malfonia."

Evan cast a glance at Alex. They both nodded slightly. Then they both began to walk forward like zombies, pretending their helmets were controlling them.

"Guard the crystal," Alex said.

Evan and Alex walked into the dome and stood on each side of the crystal. The aliens looked pleased.

"And now," said the first alien, "it is time to begin our invasion!"

"Not so fast, dude!" Alex cried. He picked up the crystal and hurled it to the concrete basement floor. Pieces of the crystal flaked off, scattering everywhere.

"Nooooooo!" cried the aliens.

Evan jumped out of the dome and joined Alex. Together, they banged the crystal again and again.

The aliens shrieked in terror—and then, suddenly, they vanished.

Go to page 38.

Continued from page 135

Evan was about to sneak into the house when he remembered a thought he had earlier in the day.

Patience is the key to a good investigation.

Patience had got him this far, Evan realized. It would be silly to rush into the house without knowing more about the Snyggs. For all he knew, he could be running into danger.

Evan quickly left the Snyggs' house and ran up to his bedroom. There, sitting at his desk, he thought up his plan.

Since the Snyggs moved in, Evan's mom had been bugging him to make friends with Simon. Evan hadn't really wanted to. He missed Dave, and wasn't looking to find a replacement. Besides, Simon had seemed a little . . . weird.

Of course the Snyggs are weird, Evan scribbled into his notebook. *They're monsters or aliens or something!*

To find out for sure, Evan would have to get closer to the Snyggs. Pretending to be friends with Simon was the first place to start.

And so the next morning, after breakfast, Evan found himself standing at the Snyggs' front door. He started to knock, but stopped when he heard muffled voices inside.

Evan couldn't resist. He took his sound amplifier off of his belt and held it up to the door. Mr. Snygg was talking. ". . . taking over the planet," he was saying.

"We must act quickly," said a female voice. It had to be Mrs. Snygg. "We don't want them to know our true identity."

Evan gasped. Taking over the planet? True identity?

The Snyggs were aliens in disguise! He was sure of it now.

Then a third voice buzzed in the microphone: "Good-bye, Mother and Father. I will see you after school."

Simon! Evan quickly clipped the microphone back to his belt. Then he knocked on the door.

Mrs. Snygg opened the door and gave Evan a big smile. She wore a crisp blue dress with a white apron on top. Her yellow-blonde hair hung straight to her shoulders and then curled up at the ends. "Why, hello, boy from next door," she said.

"H-hello," Evan said, all the while thinking, *I'm talking to an alien!* "Is Simon home?"

Before she could answer, Simon poked out his head from behind his mom. "Hello, Evan Kim," he said, holding out his hand.

Evan realized Simon wanted a handshake. He

shook Simon's hand. It felt clammy and cold to the touch. "I was wondering if you, uh, if you want to walk to school together," Evan said, trying to sound as innocent as possible.

"I would be pleased to," Simon said, and he stepped out of the door.

What a weird thing to say, Evan thought.

He and Simon walked to the sidewalk in silence. Evan slyly tried to study the boy as they walked.

Everything about Simon looked brand-new. His white basketball sneakers didn't have a single mark or scuff. His jeans, the kind those kids in the skateboarding commercial wore, were bright blue. His T-shirt, emblazoned with the name of the local baseball team, looked like it had been ironed.

Even Simon's face looked new, in a weird way. His red hair was plastered neatly against his head, without a hair out of place. Even his freckles looked perfect—three little brown dots on each cheek.

"So, Simon," Evan said casually. "Where did you and your family move from?"

"We moved from Kansas," Simon said matter-of-factly.

"Oh, really?" Evan asked. "I thought you maybe moved from somewhere far away. Like, *really* far away."

"No," Simon said, still smiling. "We are from Kansas."

They were getting closer to the school now. Evan decided to dig a little deeper. "So, what do you like to do?" he asked.

"I like to play baseball," Simon answered. "And eat apple pie."

Hmm. That sounded normal enough. Maybe *too* normal. Evan tried one more time.

"You know, I saw this cool special on TV the other day," he said. "It was about alien life on other planets. I think there are probably aliens out there—don't you?"

Simon stopped walking. He turned and looked Evan in the face. His smile never wavered. "Do not be silly, Evan Kim," Simon said. "There are no such things as aliens."

Evan kept an eye on Simon all morning. Everything he did seemed suspicious. Like how he never yawned or fidgeted once. He never asked to use the bathroom. And during science, when Mr. Rieder asked if anyone knew how far Earth was from the sun, Simon knew it was 150 million kilometers.

Evan started adding up the evidence in his head. Simon talked weird, dressed weird, and acted weird. That wasn't exactly enough to prove he was an alien, but then of course, there was the spyglass. Simon was hiding his alien form some-how, and only the spyglass could reveal his true form. All of those things added up to pretty convincing proof, as far as Evan was concerned, but he still wanted more.

When it came time for lunch, Evan invited Simon to sit with him and Billy and Todd at their usual table. Billy and Todd didn't seem to care. They were too busy playing with their handheld video games to do more than nod and grunt at Simon when he sat down.

Meanwhile, Evan eyed Simon's neatly folded paper lunch bag. "Hey, Simon," Evan said. "What do you have for lunch? Wanna trade?"

"I have a peanut butter and jelly sandwich," Simon said.

"Cool," Evan said. He switched bags with Simon before the other boy could object.

Evan opened the bag and took out a sandwich neatly wrapped in plastic. It looked normal on the outside, at least.

Evan unwrapped the sandwich and lifted open the bread.

A layer of jelly had been carefully applied to the bread.

So had a layer of creamy white butter. And another layer of peanuts, still in their shells.

Peanuts. Butter. And jelly.

"Aha!" Evan shouted, rising to his feet. "This proves it! Only an alien would have a sandwich like this!"

Simon looked at Evan, stunned. Billy and Todd looked up from their video games.

"Dude," Billy said. "What are you, crazy or something?"

Evan cringed. He had lost control, and now his investigation was in jeopardy. He had to find a way to make things right.

If Evan gives Billy and Todd the spyglass to prove that he's right, go to page 81.

If Evan decides to act like he was just joking, go to page 114.

Continued from page 44

"This is too weird—even for me," Evan said.

Evan took the helmet downstairs and threw it in the outside garbage can. The next day, after school, he returned the spyglass to Sebastian Cream's Junk Shop.

The next few weeks were fairly quiet. Evan quit his spy route and started playing video games after school with Billy and Todd again. When he wasn't playing games, he sat in front of the TV, watching cartoons.

A cartoon cat and mouse were chasing each other around the screen one Saturday morning as Evan watched, munching on cereal. Then the picture went black, and a news bulletin popped up on the screen.

"An alien invasion has begun!" the newscaster was saying. "It seems that aliens have been monitoring our brain waves for several years now, preparing for the attack. Right now, Earth is surrounded by alien spacecraft!"

Evan frowned and hit the channel button on the remote. This had to be some kind of joke. But the same news bulletin appeared on every channel.

Then Evan heard the sound of screams coming from outside. He raced out onto his front lawn.

Hundreds of dark, alien spaceships hovered in

the sky overhead, like a flock of predatory birds waiting to strike.

"Oh, no," Evan moaned. "Those helmet heads were right all along!"

THE END

Continued from page 74

"Let's hear Evan's plan," Betsy said. "He's been pretty smart about things so far."

But Evan chickened out. "It might not work. Maybe we should just take apart the machine instead."

"Let's do it!" Alex yelled.

The UFO Society members descended on the machine, yanking on tubes and kicking the metal pieces. But for a machine that looked like it was made of junk, it was surprisingly well-built. Evan tugged and tugged at a clump of wires, but they wouldn't come loose.

Looking around, Evan saw the others weren't faring much better. The machine looked pretty much like it had when they'd started.

"Dude, maybe we should try your plan," Alex said.

Evan looked at the digital clock. 00:00:15.

Only fifteen seconds left.

"I think it's too late," Evan said, fear rising within him.

Everyone watched, frozen with fear, as the numbers counted down.

10 . . . 9 . . . 8 . . . 7 . . . 6 . . . 5 . . . 4 . . . 3 . . . 2 . . . 1 . . .

As the number 0 flashed, the large crystal

began to glow again. An alien materialized inside the dome. But this was no hologram. This one was real. It stepped outside the dome into the basement.

Behind it, another alien materialized. Then another. Soon, a dozen aliens stood in front of the machine.

"Greetings, humans," said the first alien. "We are the Malfonians. You have the honor of becoming our first prisoners."

"Not without a fight!" Alex said, charging forward. Evan and the others ran forward, too. It couldn't end like this. It wasn't fair!

The aliens didn't make a move. Instead, they closed their eyes.

Immediately, Evan stopped. He couldn't move. He looked down to find that his feet were bound in some kind of metal cuffs. His hands were trapped in the cuffs, too.

"You will learn soon enough," said the first alien. "There is no escape from the Malfonians."

Evan groaned. Beside him, Alex shook his head. "Whoa, dude," Alex said. "What a bummer!"

THE END

Continued from page 49

"I got a bad feeling from the mayor," Evan said. "Didn't you, Simon?"

"Yes I did, Evan Kim," Simon agreed.

Mrs. Snygg nodded. "I think you may be right. I will send a message to Paxus 4 that we are breaking protocol. We will go to the mayor's office and see what is happening."

Evan was relieved that the Snyggs had decided to help right away—even though he was curious to see their planet.

Evan told his parents he was eating dinner at the Snyggs.' They were happy he was making friends with the new neighbor kid, so they said no problem. When he got back to the Snyggs' house, he saw that each Snygg was packing a knapsack with small golden spheres. They looked like the beads of bath lotion that his sister Tina used. "What are they for?" Evan asked.

"We are a peaceful people," explained Mr. Snygg. "But these are weapons, of a sort. They will immobilize the Blorgs long enough for us to capture them."

Soon, each Snygg had a knapsack filled with the golden spheres.

"Okay, then," said Mrs. Snygg. "Let us boogie!"

Evan rode with the Snyggs to Town Hall. They parked a few blocks away and walked to the building.

Crowds of people were entering Town Hall. Evan was puzzled at first, until he noticed a sign on the front lawn:

TOWN HALL MEETING TONIGHT
7 p.m.

"What is this?" Mrs. Snygg asked.

"It happens once a month," Evan explained. "People from town come to complain to the mayor about stuff that bothers them."

"Maybe we should leave," said Mr. Snygg.

"I don't know," Evan said. "What if the mayor is planning to do something at the meeting? I think we should check it out."

The Snyggs agreed. They entered Town Hall and followed the crowd to the meeting room. They found seats on folding chairs in the back.

"So many people, Evan Kim," Simon whispered. "Do you think they are Blorgs?"

Evan remembered the spyglass. "I know how we can find out," he said.

Evan raised the spyglass to his eye and looked around the room. About half of the people there were regular humans.

The rest were Blorgs. They all seemed to be sitting on the perimeter of the crowd—almost like they were blocking in the non-aliens.

"Let me see," said Simon. He looked through the spyglass. Then he handed it to his parents.

Mr. and Mrs. Snygg took turns looking. They both seemed concerned.

"The Blorgs appear to be in attack formation," Mrs. Snygg whispered. "Perhaps we should demobilize them."

Mr. Snygg and Simon nodded. They each took out one of the gold spheres.

Mr. Snygg aimed a sphere at the nearest Blorg, who sat in the back row.

The sphere traveled swiftly but smoothly through the air, as if it was propelled by its own power. It snaked around and smacked against the back of the Blorg's neck.

Immediately, the Blorg slumped over as though he was in a deep sleep.

"Cool!" Evan said.

The mayor got in front of the crowd and started the meeting. People asked questions about backed-up sewers and streets with no stop signs.

All the while, the Snyggs slowly and carefully blasted the Blorgs, one by one.

"Can I try?" Evan asked Simon.

"Yes," he responded. "Although I am not sure

it will work. The energy field of the spheres are specifically tuned to the energy of my people. We—"

Evan didn't wait for Simon to finish. He was too excited to try out a sphere. He grabbed one from Simon's bag and then looked through the spyglass. There was a tall Blorg in the front row. A perfect target.

Evan aimed and threw the sphere. The tiny ball zigzagged through the crowd in a series of jagged motions, not at all the way the balls had moved when the Snyggs threw them.

"I guess it does not work for humans," Simon said.

Luckily, the crowd had not seen the ball yet. Evan left his seat and ran along the aisle, following the ball. If only he could grab it . . .

Suddenly, the ball took a sharp turn. It zipped up in front of Mayor Jones and hovered in front of his head.

The mayor grinned. He quickly grabbed the sphere with his fist. Then he threw it to the floor and squashed it with his foot.

"Ladies and gentlemen of Bleaktown," the mayor said, speaking into his microphone, "I'm afraid that spies have infiltrated our town meeting!" He looked right at the Snyggs in the back row.

Evan felt terrible. This was all his fault. He had to do something.

If Evan tells everyone that the mayor is really an alien, go to page 90.

If Evan distracts the crowd so the Snyggs can escape, go to page 127.

Continued from page 11

Evan decided to wait until tomorrow. He liked to stick to a routine every day. It usually bugged him when things didn't go according to schedule.

Still, during school the next day, he was more excited than ever to go on his spy route. At lunchtime, while his friends Billy and Todd played with their handheld video games, Evan took out his notebook and sketched out a new route.

He hadn't tried Bleaktown Park yet. All kinds of people could be found in the park in the afternoon. And Town Hall was near the park. That could be interesting, too.

When the final bell rang, Evan sprinted out the door and jogged toward the park. It took about fifteen minutes to get there.

The park was shaped like a long rectangle and was surrounded by streets on all four sides. A metal archway marked the entrance at one short end of the rectangle. Across the park, at the opposite short end, sat Town Hall.

Evan decided to walk around the perimeter and find a good place to settle in and spy on people. He had walked all the way up one side of the park when something caught his eye.

The first was a white building sandwiched in

between a dry cleaner's store and a dentist's office. The black-and-white sign over the door read, *Universal Fruit Outlet*. But there was no sign of fruit anywhere.

Pretty weird, thought Evan. He was looking for a bush to hide behind when something else made him stop.

A man in a blue business suit was getting out of a car on the curb. He was carrying a heavy box.

That wasn't particularly unusual, except that the man was Patrick Jones, Bleaktown's new mayor. He had taken over the office after a special election a few weeks ago.

Evan wondered what was in the box. Of course, he could spy on the mayor and find out.

If Evan spies on the Universal Fruit Outlet, go to page 12.

If Evan spies on Mayor Jones, go to page 119.

"Dude, we did it!" Alex yelled. He gave Evan a high five.

Evan was very relieved that the aliens were gone.

"That was wonderful," Betsy said, beaming. "We should all be very proud."

"Well, I think we've had enough excitement for one day," Alex said.

"That's for sure," Evan agreed.

"Why don't we meet back here tomorrow for a celebration party?" Betsy suggested.

"That sounds like a great idea!" Evan said. "But we should also prepare ourselves for another invasion. You never know when those aliens will come back!"

The friends agreed, and planned to meet the next day.

Evan got patted on the back again and again as he walked upstairs and headed toward the door. He felt totally great—like a hero or something.

Evan was thinking of ideas for tomorrow's meeting when he heard a voice behind him.

"Evan, wait up!"

Evan turned around. Kelly ran up to him. "That was great back there," she said.

"Thanks," Evan replied.

"You know, I was wondering," Kelly said as they walked. "How did you know there was alien technology in those helmets?"

Evan stopped and unclipped the spyglass. "It was this," he explained. "When I looked through it, I could see the alien technology inside."

Evan held the spyglass to his eye.

Then he gasped.

The spyglass was pointed at Kelly. But he didn't see Kelly through the lens.

He saw a gray alien with big black eyes.

Evan started to back up. "You're a . . . one of them."

"Yes, it's true," Kelly said, hanging her head. "I'm a Malfonian. My commander sent me here to infiltrate the UFO Society. I'm the one who put the technology in the helmets."

Evan started to run, but something held him back. Kelly might be an alien, but she didn't seem like the others.

"The more time I spent on Earth, the more I liked it here," Kelly went on. "I like movies. And ice cream. And kittens. We don't have any of those things on Malfonia. I'm glad the invasion failed!"

"Really?" Evan said.

Kelly nodded. "I'm going to stay on Earth. You

won't mind having a Malfonian for a friend, will you?"

Evan thought about it for a minute. Kelly might be an alien, but she wasn't any stranger than his friends Billy and Todd. In fact, she was more normal than they were in a lot of ways. "No problem," Evan said, smiling.

THE END

Continued from page 99

Evan thought about running, but something inside him was still curious. The girl looked normal enough. She wore her blonde hair in two braids down her back—and she was carrying her helmet, not wearing it.

"Hey," the girl said when she reached Evan. "I'm Kelly. Nice job getting out of there. Those alien stories are wacky, aren't they?"

Evan nodded, relieved. The girl just seemed like she wanted to talk. "So what were you doing there?"

Kelly frowned. "My parents joined a few months ago. Now they drag me there for meetings all the time. It's really boring. I told them I was coming out to find you, but I'm not going back there. It feels great to be out. Wanna go to the park?"

Evan hadn't been to the park, just to have fun, in ages. He found himself nodding his head. "Sure," he said.

He and Kelly sat on the swings, talking about the people at the UFO meeting.

"How about that lady who thinks there's an alien in her garbage disposal?" Kelly asked, giggling.

"Or the guy who thinks his dog is an alien spy?" Evan added.

"And these helmets!" Kelly cried. "I feel like such a dork in this." She put her helmet on her head. "Aliens are everywhere!" She giggled.

Evan put on his helmet, too. "Protect your brain waves!" he cried.

And then everything got fuzzy.

The next thing Evan knew, he was in his bedroom. The helmet was resting on his pillowcase. He had no idea how he'd gotten home.

A loose memory swirled around in his brain, but Evan knew it was slipping away.

Focus, Evan, he told himself. *Remember!*

Evan closed his eyes and tried hard to piece the memory together. Very slowly, a picture began to form.

He and Kelly had left the park. They had traveled to the store downtown. A store filled with . . .

. . . rocks, Evan remembered excitedly. Gemstones and crystals and things. When the shop owner wasn't looking, he and Kelly had grabbed a crystal as big as a watermelon and run out of the shop.

That's all he could remember. He squeezed his eyes shut tighter and tried to think. Then Evan remembered that they had gone back to the UFO building. They had gone into the basement . . .

That was it. He couldn't remember anything else.

"It's the helmet," Evan said, feeling certain. "It made me do something I can't remember! I never should have put it back on."

Evan picked up the helmet and examined every inch of it. It still looked like a bike helmet covered in foil. He tried to peel off the layers of foil, but they wouldn't budge. He frowned. There had to be some way to find out the real deal about the helmets.

On a hunch, Evan unclipped the spyglass from his belt. It was a pretty strong tool. Sure, it was used for distance viewing, but maybe . . .

Evan held the spyglass up to his eye and focused it on the helmet.

Then he gasped.

The spyglass was acting like some kind of X-ray, presenting him with a clear view of the helmet's insides. Evan couldn't believe what he was seeing.

A mass of strange, fluorescent tubes covered the inside of the helmet like strands of glowing spaghetti. The tubes constantly changed color from green, to blue, to pink, to yellow.

Evan wasn't sure what it was. Some kind of new technology, maybe. He was sure it had caused his strange behavior this afternoon.

To find out more, Evan knew he would have to go back to the UFO Society. But what he really wanted to do was forget all about that place—and go back to his normal life.

If Evan vows never to go back to the UFO Society, go to page 27.

If Evan decides to keep investigating, go to page 139.

Continued from page 17

"You run to the left, and I'll run to the right," Evan told Simon. Simon nodded and took off.

Evan sped down the length of the building and ran to the front. Simon charged around the opposite corner of the building. Evan pointed toward the park and sped across the street.

Before entering the park, Evan snuck a quick look behind him. The aliens were good climbers, but not such good runners. He and Simon had a pretty big lead.

Simon caught up to Evan, and they ran across the park, darting between moms with baby carriages and kids playing catch. When they reached the end of the park, Evan headed down a side street, toward one of the shortcuts he knew from his spy route. They cut across some backyards and finally ended up in an alley behind Main Street. For the first time, Evan stopped to catch his breath.

"I think we lost them," Evan finally said.

Simon nodded. "You are pretty good, Evan Kim."

"So, what now?" Evan asked. "Spying on them ourselves doesn't seem like such a good idea anymore."

"Yes," Simon said. "You are right. I think we

should go to my house. My parents will know what to do."

Evan raised an eyebrow. "Your parents? Won't they think we're crazy if we start talking about aliens?"

Simon grinned. "No, I do not think so."

As they walked home, Evan kept looking over his shoulder for the men in business suits. The coast was clear. The boys relaxed and slowed their pace.

Soon, they came to Simon and Evan's block. Evan followed Simon into the Snyggs' house. The door opened up into a large living room. A white rug covered the floor, blending in with the white walls. The two couches in the room were white with gleaming metal arms and legs. A metal and glass coffee table separated the couches.

Mr. and Mrs. Snygg sat on one of the couches. Mrs. Snygg wore a crisp blue dress. Her yellow-blonde hair bounced on her shoulders. Mr. Snygg looked like a taller version of Simon, except that he wore a black business suit and a blue tie.

The Snyggs stood up when the boys came in.

"Hello, Simon," said Mrs. Snygg. "Who is your nice friend?"

"This is Evan Kim from next door," Simon said.

Mr. Snygg held out his hand for Evan to shake. It felt rather cold and clammy.

Simon turned to Evan. "If you don't mind, I need to speak to my parents for a moment," he said.

"Sure," Evan said, shrugging. The Snyggs walked through a door into what looked like a kitchen. Evan sat down on one of the couches.

He wondered what the Snyggs were talking about. For a second, he thought about using his microphone to find out, but decided that wouldn't be right. The Snyggs had invited him into their home. Spying on them would just be weird.

A few minutes later, the Snyggs came through the door. They all had big grins on their faces.

"Simon has just told us what happened," Mr. Snygg said.

"And you believe us?" Evan asked.

The Snyggs looked at each other, then nodded. Mr. Snygg, Mrs. Snygg, and Simon each pressed a button on the wristwatches they wore.

The Snyggs' bodies started to flicker, like the way a picture moves when a videotape gets stuck in a recorder, Evan thought. Then their bodies started to change. The picture stopped flickering.

Now the three Snyggs looked like aliens: one tall, one medium-sized, and one short. Each alien wore a silver space suit. Green hands and feet stuck out of the suits. Two huge, dark eyes were set into each green face. And a mass of long, green tentacles wiggled and squiggled on top of each alien's head.

"Aaaaaaaaah!" Evan screamed. "You're aliens, too! Just like the mayor!"

He ran to the door and started pulling at the doorknob, but the door was locked.

The tallest alien shook his head. Evan guessed this was Mr. Snygg. "We are aliens, yes. But not like Mayor Jones. He and the others are from the planet Blorg. They are from a warrior planet and they want to take over the universe."

Evan slowly turned around. Mr. Snygg might be telling the truth. The Snyggs didn't look like those other alien guys, at least.

"We are from the planet Paxus 4," said Simon, the smallest alien. "We keep peace throughout the galaxy. We followed the Blorg trail to your town and have been spying on them."

That could be true, too, Evan thought. He and Simon had both been spying on the mayor. "So what do we do now?" he asked.

"All peace missions must follow a certain procedure," said Mrs. Snygg. "Now that we know that the Blorg leader has established a base here, we will return to our planet and make a report. They will send more Paxons to stop the Blorg invasion."

"Mother says you may come with us if you want, Evan," Simon said. "We will be back by tomorrow."

Evan couldn't believe what he was hearing. He had just been invited to visit another planet! He bet no other kid on Earth had done that before.

But then he remembered Mayor Jones.

"That would be cool," Evan said. "But do you have to go back to your planet right now? The way the mayor was talking, the Blorgs were going to invade Earth any minute."

Mr. and Mrs. Snygg looked at each other and frowned.

"We can only abandon proper procedure in an emergency," Mr. Snygg said. "If you think it is important, we will stay and fight."

If Evan goes to the Snyggs' planet, go to page 54.

If Evan convinces the Snyggs to stay and fight, go to page 31.

Continued from page 135

Evan ran to the back of the Snyggs' house. Next to the back door, just a few inches above the ground, was a small window that looked into the basement. Evan and Dave used the window to sneak in and out of Dave's house sometimes, just for fun.

But this isn't fun, Evan told himself solemnly. *This is serious. Aliens could be in there!*

Evan knelt down and pulled at the window frame. The hinges had rusted long ago, so you could pull out the whole frame and then just push it back in when you were done.

Evan stuck his feet through the small opening. There was about a five-foot drop to the ground, he remembered, but it wasn't so bad if you landed on your feet. He leaned back and slipped his legs through the window, slowly inching the rest of his body through. Then he jumped into the dark basement.

Squish!

Evan frowned. He didn't remember anything squishy on Dave's basement floor before. He tried to move his feet, but they were stuck in some kind of sticky goo. He took the flashlight off of his belt and shined the light around him.

He was standing in the middle of some kind of

giant plant pod. Three large, open petals surrounded him. Green slime dripped down the petals into the center of the pod, sticking to his feet like glue. He tried to move his feet again, but they wouldn't budge.

"Hello?" Evan called out. He didn't care if the Snyggs were aliens or not—this pod thing was totally creeping him out.

Evan tried to move his feet again, then smacked himself on the forehead. "Of course!" he said. "I'll just step out of my shoes."

He bent down to untie his sticky shoelaces.

Squeeeeeeeeee . . .

The plant petals were moving now, starting to close like a flower bud during a spring rain.

"No!" Evan cried, yanking at his shoelaces.

But it was no use. The petals closed tightly, trapping Evan inside the pod. He felt the green slime plop into his hair and ooze down the back of his shirt. He furiously pounded on the petals, but his arms only got stuck in the slime.

"Help!" Evan screamed.

But no one heard him cry out.

THE END

The door opened into a large room with freshly painted white walls. A rickety wood table held two boxes of doughnuts, a bottle of apple juice, and some paper cups. Metal folding chairs, arranged in a circle, held an assortment of people. There was the old woman and the two men in business suits Evan had seen enter, along with about thirty other people who looked pretty average—except for the fact that they all wore silver helmets.

"This is—what's your name, dude?" Alex asked.

"Evan," Evan replied, then immediately wished he had used a fake name. What kind of a spy was he?

"This is Evan's first meeting," Alex continued. "He needs a helmet."

"Welcome, Evan," everyone said at once.

The gray-haired woman walked up and handed Evan a helmet. "Here you go, young man," she said, smiling sweetly.

"Thanks," Evan said. "But I mean—well, this is my first meeting and all—what exactly is the helmet for?"

Alex laughed. "To keep your brain waves safe, dude," he said, "from the aliens."

Aliens? Evan wasn't sure he had heard right.

"Yes," said the old lady. "That's what the UFO Society is all about. Keeping the world safe from aliens."

Then it clicked. UFO Society. <u>U</u>niversal <u>F</u>ruit <u>O</u>utlet. Of course! This was one of those weird groups of people who believed in aliens and stuff.

"Why don't you have a seat, dear?" said the old lady. "The meeting is about to start."

If Evan thinks the UFO Society is too nutty for him and decides to leave, go to page 60.

If Evan sticks around to find out what the UFO Society is all about, go to page 98.

"I guess it couldn't hurt to go back to your planet for a night," Evan said. "It will probably take more than just us to stop a whole Blorg invasion."

"Do you think you will come with us?" Simon asked.

"I'd like to, but what will I tell my mom?" Evan replied.

Simon's tentacles wriggled as he thought. "You could tell her we are going . . . camping!"

The Snyggs hit their wristwatch buttons and returned to their human forms. Mrs. Snygg and Evan went to Evan's house and talked to his mom. Happy that Evan had made a new friend, Mrs. Kim agreed to the camping trip.

Evan felt a twinge of guilt about lying to his mom, but he convinced himself it was for the best. After all, he was helping save the planet.

So, about an hour later, Evan found himself in the Snyggs' garage, staring at what looked like a giant gold ball. "Is that your spaceship?" Evan asked.

"Sort of," Simon said. "Our craft doesn't travel so much through space as it does through time. It's easier than dodging meteors and zigzagging around planets."

"Wow," Evan said. He didn't really understand it, but it sounded impressive.

Before they boarded the craft, Mrs. Snygg gave Evan a wristwatch of his own. "Press the red button," she said.

Evan did, and heard a strange, faint buzzing in his ears. Then he saw that his hands had turned into green claws! Evan looked up and caught his reflection in the gold spacecraft. He looked just like the Snyggs! "Am I an alien now?" Evan asked, slightly panicked.

Simon laughed. "No. You just look like one. Your human form might be frightening to the citizens of Paxus 4."

Evan had not thought of that before. If the Snyggs looked scary to him, then it made sense that he looked scary to them, too.

The Snyggs returned to their alien forms, and they all boarded the giant golden ball. Four seats faced a sort of pillar in the center of the sphere. Evan sat in one of the seats, and Mrs. Snygg strapped a kind of seat belt across his chest. "Don't worry. It should be a smooth ride," she said.

Then Mr. Snygg held his hand over the top of the pillar. A sudden darkness swept over the craft, but the pillar started to glow with golden light. A high-pitched hum filled the sphere, causing

Evan's chair to vibrate.

A few seconds later, light returned to the craft. Mr. Snygg took his hand off the pillar. "We're here," he said cheerfully.

The door of the craft slid open, and Evan followed the Snyggs out into a large, rectangular room.

"Welcome to our home," Mrs. Snygg said. "You boys wait here. We must address the Paxus council quickly and tell them what has happened."

While Mr. and Mrs. Snygg were gone, Simon gave Evan a tour of the house. He showed Evan his bedroom, which was packed with the Paxus version of comic books. They looked like regular comics, but the pictures in the panels moved and talked. Evan met Simon's pet, a furry little ball that flew around the room and made a weird croaking noise. They ate *farna*, a food that looked like an apple, but tasted like pizza. And Simon showed Evan Paxon television, translating all the funny parts into English.

"So, how do you like our planet?" Simon asked.

"It's a lot of fun," Evan replied. "But it kind of makes me miss Earth. I hope the Blorgs don't take us over."

At that moment, a door slid open, and Mr. and Mrs. Snygg walked in. Evan wasn't sure, but he thought he saw a sad look on their alien faces.

Simon must have seen it, too. "What's wrong?" he asked.

Mr. Snygg walked to the television and pressed a button. Now, a picture of Earth filled the screen. Red, scary-looking spaceships had surrounded the planet.

"The Blorgs have begun their invasion," Mr. Snygg said sadly. "Their forces are much more powerful than we'd thought. There is nothing we can do."

Evan suddenly felt like there was a rock in his stomach. "What do you mean?" he asked.

Mrs. Snygg put an arm around Evan's shoulder. "We will have to wait and see," she said. "At least you are safe here with us, Evan."

The truth slowly crept over Evan. "You mean . . ."

Simon nodded. "You might have to stay here with us forever!"

THE END

Continued from page 80

The clock counted down. The members of the UFO Society started to whisper, then chatter, then yell as they decided what to do.

Betsy Walker quieted things down with a sharp whistle. "We've got to do something," she said. "If this machine is bringing some kind of alien force to Earth, then we have to stop it. It's our duty."

"Red means stop," Alex said, pointing to the red button. "Maybe it will stop the machine."

"Red also means you should keep away from something," Evan pointed out. "I think we should press the blue button instead."

A murmur went up among the Society members.

"Evan was smart enough to figure out the helmets," Betsy said. "I think we should trust him."

Evan hoped he was right. Blue was just a guess—nothing more. With trembling hands, he pressed the blue button.

Immediately, the colored wires and tubes sticking out of the towers began to glow. The machine began to shake.

Evan's stomach sank. He had pressed the wrong button. They were doomed!

"Get back, dude," Alex said, dragging him toward the stairs.

Evan watched as a blue glow enveloped the machine. Then, in the next instant, the machine simply vanished.

The basement was eerily quiet. Evan rubbed his eyes. Had the machine really disappeared?

"You did it, dude," Alex said. The crowd in the basement let out a cheer.

"Good work, Evan," said Betsy. "It looks like we have stopped the aliens' plans—for now. But we will have to be vigilant. We cannot rest until we uncover the truth. Will you help us?"

Evan thought about this. The UFO people were a little nutty—but they had been right about the aliens. There was important work to do now, and he wanted to be part of it. "Sure," Evan replied. "On one condition."

"What's that?" Betsy asked.

Evan smiled. "No more helmets!"

Go to page 107.

Continued from page 53

"If it's okay with you, I think I'll forget about the meeting," Evan said. This was just a little too strange for him.

Alex and the gray-haired woman didn't seem to mind at all. Evan started to hand back the helmet, but the old lady pushed it back into his arms. "Keep it, dear," she said. "You never know when you'll need it!"

Evan shrugged and tucked the helmet under his arm. Then he left the UFO Society and headed straight home. He couldn't wait to write a full report about this. It was definitely his most interesting find yet.

When he got home, he found his dad in the kitchen, chopping vegetables, while his mom was stirring something on the stove.

"Hi, honey," Mrs. Kim said. But her eyes narrowed when she saw the helmet.

"What's that?" she asked.

"It's supposed to keep aliens from reading your brain waves," Evan said. "Can you believe that? I mean, who actually thinks aliens are real?"

Mr. and Mrs. Kim exchanged worried glances. Then they nodded.

"Evan, sit down," Mr. Kim said. "Your mom and I have to tell you something."

Uh oh, Evan thought. *This can't be good.*

Mrs. Kim took a deep breath. "Now that you're twelve, it's time you know the truth," she said. "We are all aliens, Evan. You, me, your father. We were sent here to read the brain waves of humans and report back to our home planet, Miramax."

Evan was stunned for a second. Then he burst out laughing. "Very funny, Mom. Is today April Fools' Day, or something?"

Evan's parents frowned.

"This is very serious, Evan," said Mr. Kim. "You are now old enough to join the mission. It's very important."

Evan couldn't believe what he was hearing. He started to panic. His parents seemed deadly serious. He stood up, nearly knocking over his chair. "It's not true!" he cried. "We're not aliens! We're human!"

Mr. Kim pointed to Evan's belt. "If you don't believe me, use the alien detector there."

Alien detector? What was his dad talking about? Then Evan realized his dad was pointing to the spyglass.

"Okay," Evan said suspiciously. Things were getting stranger and stranger. Were his parents working with Sebastian Cream somehow? It was the only explanation.

Evan unclipped the spyglass. He held it up to his eye and focused it on his parents.

Two gray aliens with large black eyes stared back at him, smiling. "We told you so, Evan," they said.

THE END

Continued from page 142

Evan didn't want to have to push around a little old lady. But he figured it would be the easiest way out.

"Catch!" Evan cried, throwing his helmet into the startled crowd of UFO Society members. Then he dodged, running toward Betsy. "Sorry, but I really need to get out of here!"

The gray-haired woman's eyes narrowed. Then she held her arms out in front of her, elbows bent, in some kind of martial-arts pose.

"Hiiiiiiiyaaaaaaaaah!" Betsy cried. Then she sprang into the air like an action hero, her right leg extended.

"Whoa!" Evan ducked. Losing his balance, he tumbled to the floor.

The next thing he knew, Betsy was crouched on his chest, pinning his shoulders to the floor like a wrestler. "Stop the intruder," Betsy said calmly.

"Okay! You win!" Evan said. "You stopped me. What are you going to do with me?"

Betsy released her grip on Evan's shoulders.

Alex walked up behind her. "You have discovered our secret," he said. "These humans think they are protecting themselves from our powers with these helmets. Instead, we are using them to control their minds."

Evan realized that although Alex was talking, there was really some kind of alien presence behind his words.

"That's pretty clever of you," Evan said, trying to find a way out of this mess. "I think what you're doing is great. So why don't you let me go?"

"You know too much," Alex said. "And our invasion is slated to begin very soon. We need to keep you under control until it happens."

The members of the UFO Society picked up Evan by his arms and legs. They carried him through the back door, down a long hallway, and then dumped him in a closet, locking the door behind them.

Evan slumped to the ground and sighed. "I wish I'd never come back to this place!" he moaned.

THE END

Continued from page 104

Evan decided to impress the agents.

"I'd whip off my disguise, and tell all the Wiznuts to freeze!" Evan said confidently. "If they tried to resist, I'd fight my way out of there."

The two agents looked at each other. Agent 33 shook her head.

"The Wiznuts are normally peaceful, but they quickly retaliate against any act of aggression," Agent 564 explained. "Your actions would lead to interplanetary war! The answer would be to simply run away. Wiznuts are extremely slow."

Evan sighed. He should have just told the truth!

Agent 33 stood up. "I'm sorry, Evan," she said. "We can't afford to have any hotheaded agents on our team." She unhooked one of the gadgets from her belt. It looked kind of like a walkie-talkie with an antennae. Agent 33 took some earplugs off of her belt and stuffed them in her ears. Agent 564 did the same. Then Agent 33 aimed the antennae right at Evan.

"Uh, what are you going to do with that?" Evan asked suspiciously.

"You know too much, Evan," she replied. "Don't worry. This won't hurt a bit."

"Wait!" Evan cried. "I was going to say that I would run from the Wiznuts. I just wanted to impress—"

Evan opened his eyes. Clouds floated in the blue sky overhead. He felt stiff and sleepy, like he had been taking a nap.

Evan realized he was on a park bench, lying on his back. He slowly sat up. His head felt like it was filled with cotton candy.

Evan tried to think. After school, he had gone on his spy route. He saw Mayor Jones carrying a big box into Town Hall . . .

He couldn't remember anything after that. Not a thing.

"Weird," Evan said. He had no idea what had happened. He had a vague idea that it had something to do with the spyglass.

Evan touched his belt to retrieve the spyglass.

It was gone.

Panicked, Evan hopped off of the bench. He looked under the seat, in the weeds, behind a nearby tree. The spyglass was nowhere to be found.

"Oh, well," Evan reasoned. "I must have spied on the mayor, got bored, and then took a nap. I guess nothing exciting happened."

That had to be it. There was no other explanation.

Right?

THE END

Continued from page 132

Evan decided to trust Simon. Sure, he was an alien with tentacles growing out of his head. But he had been pretty nice to Evan. And there was something really creepy about Mayor Jones.

"Take that!" Evan cried. He opened the vial and tossed the contents onto Mayor Jones. A slippery gold liquid splashed on the alien's body.

"Aaaaaiiiiieeeeeeeeee!" The mayor let out a horrifying shriek. Then his whole body froze, as though it had been turned to stone.

The other Blorgs started to panic. They let go of the Snyggs, who picked up their fallen weapons. They aimed the weapons at the Blorgs. More gold liquid shot out of the weapons and splashed onto the evil aliens. One by one, their bodies froze up.

"Are they dead?" Evan asked.

"No," said Mr. Snygg. "We can give them an antidote to the poison. But first we must transport them to the interplanetary prison system."

"So the mayor was lying when he said you were going to take over the planet, too?" Evan asked, hoping he was right.

Simon nodded. "We are here to protect your planet, not conquer it. We are from the planet Paxus 4. Our job is to keep peace in the galaxy."

"Wow!" Evan said. "That's really cool."

"I'm glad you trusted me, Evan Kim," Simon

said. "If not, the Blorg leader would have escaped."

Evan felt pretty good. He had helped to stop an alien takeover of Earth. How many real spies could say they had done that?

"So, will I ever see you again?" Evan asked.

"I do not know," Simon said. "We will probably return from time to time to make sure your planet is safe. But we may have to take on new human forms. I do not know if you will recognize us."

Evan took the spyglass from his belt and looked at it. If Mr. Cream hadn't made him try it out, he never would have made friends with Simon Snygg. Or helped save the world. He was definitely going to keep the spyglass once his week was up. "Don't worry," Evan said. "If you come back, I'll find you!"

THE END

Continued from page 86

After what he had seen earlier, Evan was curious to get another look at the mayor's office. "I'll go on the computer chip mission," Evan said.

Agent 33 nodded. "Good. You'll be with me. I'll pick you up at nine o'clock tonight."

Evan frowned. "I really want to, but my parents—"

"Will not give you a problem," Agent 33 said. "You are an agent now. They will understand. We'll take care of it."

Before he left, the agents gave Evan a black suit of his own that was just his size. After dinner, Evan put it on and checked himself out in the mirror. "Not bad," Evan said. He looked like a professional spy—not just a kid with a spy kit.

Evan hooked his new spy tools to his belt and went downstairs. He wasn't sure what Agent 33 had said to his parents, but they both smiled and beamed at him as he came into the living room.

"Good luck, son," Mr. Kim said. Mrs. Kim snapped Evan's picture.

At precisely nine o'clock, a car horn honked outside. Evan walked out to find Agent 33 in a black van. He climbed into the passenger's seat.

Agent 33 explained the mission as she drove. "We know the Blorgs are planning a massive invasion of Earth," she said. "But we need more details. We believe Mayor Jones has the plans encoded on a computer chip hidden in his office. The doors and windows are guarded with Blorg alarms, so that's where you come in, Agent 12."

She took a map from her suit pocket and handed it to Evan. "The air vent marked on the left side of the building leads directly to the mayor's office," she said. "You will climb through the vent, swing down into the office, and retrieve the chip. It's hidden in the glass onion paper-weight on his desk."

"Got it," Evan said. His heart was pumping fast. This was real spy stuff. He hoped he wouldn't blow it.

Agent 33 handed him what looked like a small earplug. "Wear this at all times," she said. "It's a radio device. We will be in constant contact."

Evan nodded. Knowing he'd be in touch with Agent 33 the whole time made him feel a little better. She looked like she could do anything.

The agent pulled the van onto the side street next to Town Hall. She nodded to Evan. "Good luck, Agent 12," she said. "Don't let us down."

"I won't," Evan said, but the words came out a little shaky. He exited the van. Then he used a small flashlight to illuminate the map.

Finding the air vent shaft was easy. Luckily, it

was located above a metal dumpster. Evan climbed on top of the dumpster, took a small screwdriver from his belt, and removed the metal filter covering the air shaft.

The shaft was rectangle-shaped, and just tall and wide enough for Evan to squeeze through. He hoisted himself up and began to wriggle along the shaft, keeping the map in front of him. He followed the twists and turns to the spot Agent 33 had marked. He should be at the mayor's office now.

Evan looked through the metal slats in the grate. It was the mayor's office, all right. Everything was dark and quiet.

"I've reached the location," Evan whispered, knowing Agent 33 could hear him through the radio. "Looks clear."

"Proceed, Agent 12," came the reply.

Evan unscrewed the grate and lowered himself into the mayor's office. He shined his flashlight on the mayor's desk.

There were some papers and pens and some scattered onion peels, but no glass paperweight.

"I can't find the onion," Evan said.

"Try the desk drawers," Agent 33 responded.

Evan had started to open the top drawer, when he heard something. He froze.

He could hear the sounds of voices. They sounded close.

"Someone's in the building," Evan said.

"Get out now!" Agent 33 said. "This mission's over!"

"Right," Evan said.

But he hesitated. He was so close to completing his mission. The voices didn't sound that close. He probably had time to take a quick look in the drawers and get out without being caught.

If Evan keeps looking for the onion, go to page 111.

If Evan obeys Agent 33, go to page 105.

Continued from page 80

"Hey, doesn't red mean stop?" asked Alex. "Maybe we should press the red button."

Evan wasn't sure. But he didn't want to be the one to make the decision.

"Okay," Evan shrugged.

Alex pressed the red button. The large crystal began to glow with white light. Suddenly, an image appeared inside the dome.

It looked like an alien—the kind you see in books and on T-shirts—with large, black eyes, gray skin, and two tiny holes where a nose should be. Its long arms and legs were spindly, like branches of a tree.

Evan felt light-headed. He was looking at a real alien! Or was he? The alien's body was kind of see-through, like a . . .

"A hologram!" Alex cried. "Whoa!"

The alien hologram began to speak.

"Security has been breached," it said in a monotone voice. "Now the invasion must be sped up. Prepare for five minute countdown."

The digital numbers flashed wildly. When they stopped, they read 00:05:00.

The alien hologram vanished.

"Oh, dear," Betsy Walker said, looking rather pale. "An alien invasion. What have we done?"

The members of the UFO Society began to murmur nervously. Some of them began rushing up the stairs.

"Hey, slow down, dudes!" Alex called out. "We're the UFO Society, remember? We can't give up now. We've got to stop this invasion!"

"But how?" someone asked. "We've only got five minutes."

Alex shrugged. "I don't know. Maybe we could tear apart this machine thingy."

Evan had an idea, too, but it was risky. Still, it might work.

"I think I know a way we can trick the aliens," Evan said.

If the UFO Society decides to take apart the machine, go to page 29.

If the UFO Society agrees to try Evan's trick, go to page 18.

Continued from page 126

Evan crawled through the drainage pipe. A damp smell tickled his nose. Evan tried not to sneeze.

Agent 564 had said that the warehouse was empty, but he wasn't taking any chances. The security on the regular entrances was tight, and monitored by video cameras. He couldn't risk letting the Blorgs know that the investigators were onto them.

The pipe curved up and came to a dead end. Evan saw a round grate up ahead, marked with tiny holes. He cautiously raised his new periscope through one of the holes and looked around.

There in the center of the warehouse was a huge spaceship. It looked awesome—just like something from the movies.

Evan turned the periscope all around. No sign of life. Perfect. He could lift the grate, take some photos, and get out of there.

Evan started snapping pictures, but his curiosity tugged at him like a dog tugging on the leash. If he climbed out of the pipe, he could get great photos of the spaceship. That would really impress the agents.

So he climbed out of the pipe. He took picture after picture, stepping closer each time. Soon, Evan was standing at the bottom of the metal steps that led into the spaceship. "Wow," he said. It really was amazing.

Evan carefully stepped on the first step. Then the next. Soon, he was inside the ship.

Evan had never seen anything like it. There were all kinds of screens and control panels. Evan snapped pictures like crazy.

Suddenly, he lost his balance. He banged into one of the control panels. His elbow slammed into a black button.

At that very instant, the ship began to hum and shake. Evan ran to the door, but it quickly closed. He tried to find a lever or button to get it open, but couldn't.

Then, behind him, Evan heard a sound.

"Ten seconds to takeoff," a computer voice intoned. "10 . . . 9 . . . 8 . . . 7 . . . 6 . . . 5 . . . 4 . . ."

"No!" Evan cried. "Stop! Wait!"

"3 . . . 2 . . . 1!"

And the ship blasted through the warehouse and shot into space.

THE END

Continued from page 142

Evan couldn't bear the thought of pushing gray-haired little Betsy out of his way. He ran toward Alex instead.

"Coming through, dude!" Evan yelled. He lowered his head and charged into Alex, in a weak attempt to give him a head-butt. But his head just bounced harmlessly off of Alex's stomach.

"Stop the intruder," Alex said, reaching out toward Evan.

Suddenly, the door behind Alex opened, sending Alex tumbling backwards. Kelly stood there, a confused look on her face.

"Kelly, the helmets are making everyone crazy!" Evan said. "We've got to make everyone take off their helmets. They won't listen to me!"

Alex rose to his feet, rubbing his head. His helmet had fallen off. "Hey, did I just try to hurt you or something, dude?" he asked. "Sorry about that."

The UFO Society members looked confused now, but Evan knew it was only a matter of time before they started attacking again.

"We've got to get their helmets off," Evan said.

"No problem, dude," Alex said. He ran to the table against the wall and grabbed the box of doughnuts there. He held one up. "Stale. Good for throwing and stuff. Just watch."

Alex tossed a donut at the helmet of one of the guys in business suits. The stale doughnut knocked the helmet off of his head.

"Cool!" Alex cried.

Kelly and Evan each grabbed a handful of doughnuts and followed Alex's lead.

Bonk! Bonk! Bonk!

Soon, doughnuts were flying, sending helmets clattering to the floor.

The UFO Society members all looked like they were waking up from a nap. Alex gathered them back in a circle while Evan explained to them what he had discovered about the helmets.

"I think the helmets are controlling you, somehow," Evan finished. "You know, I didn't really believe in aliens when I came in here, but now I think something is going on."

"I think the boy is right," said Betsy. "I keep getting these strange memories. Like I've been building something . . ."

"That's what you were saying before," Evan said excitedly. "'We must build it!'"

"I remember now, dude," Alex said. "We have been building something . . . and it's in the basement."

"I didn't think we had a basement," Betsy said.

Everyone turned and looked at the back door.

"We've never opened it before, have we?" asked one man.

Alex stepped to the door. "I guess now's the time."

He opened the door, which led to a dark staircase. In single file, they walked down the stairs; Evan and Kelly were at the end of the line.

"This seems really familiar," Kelly said, shuddering.

Before he reached the bottom of the stairs, Evan heard a huge gasp. He tried to peek around the person in front of him.

Then Evan gasped, too.

A huge machine was in the center of the long, concrete basement room. Evan had never before seen anything like it. It seemed to have been put together from ordinary objects. Metal garbage cans were piled on top of one another, making two tall columns on either side. Brightly colored wires and garden hoses snaked in and out of the cans. The center of the machine was a dome shape that seemed to be covered in bubble wrap. In the center of the dome, Evan saw a huge crystal—the same crystal he and Kelly had stolen the day before.

Evan pushed through the crowd to get a closer look. A metal beam connected the two metal towers, passing in front of the dome. A collection of what looked like lawn mower and motorcycle motors were lined up on the beam. Wires traveled from the motors to a computer screen.

And on the screen were digital numbers: 07:32:02. The numbers were counting down, second by second.

"It's some kind of timer," Evan said, growing nervous. "Whatever this thing is, it's going to go off soon."

"We've got to stop it!" Alex said. He pointed to two buttons connected to the screen. "Maybe one of them will do the trick."

Evan frowned. There was one red button, and one blue button. But which one would turn off the machine?

If Evan and Alex press the red button, go to page 73.

If Evan and Alex press the blue button, go to page 58.

Continued from page 26

Evan couldn't keep things to himself any longer. If Simon and his family were planning some kind of alien takeover, he'd need some help to stop it. "I'm not crazy," he said. "Simon is an alien, and I can prove it."

Evan unclipped the spyglass from his belt. He turned to Simon. "I'm sorry to do this to you, Simon," Evan said. "But I have to think about the safety of my planet."

Evan handed the spyglass to Billy. "Just look through it," he said. "You'll see what I mean."

Billy shrugged and held the spyglass to his eye. Evan waited for Billy to scream in horror . . .

"I see Simon," Billy said. He handed the spyglass to Todd, who looked through it, too.

"What's the big deal?" Todd asked.

Evan grabbed the spyglass from him, puzzled. He looked through the lens at Simon—and saw a green alien with tentacles growing out of its head. "Don't you see it?" Evan asked, his voice rising. Then he had a horrible thought. "You must be aliens, too!"

Evan focused the spyglass on his friends, but they looked normal.

Billy shook his head and picked up his video game. "You are totally crazy, dude."

"Yeah," Todd said.

"But—but the sandwich—" Evan went to pick up the sandwich, but it was gone.

And so was Simon.

Evan plunked the spyglass on the table, disgusted. Someone was playing some kind of trick on him.

And he was pretty sure that someone was Sebastian Cream.

Go to page 109.

Continued from page 104

Evan decided to tell the truth. "I guess I'd run for it," he said.

Agent 564 stopped the watch. He turned to Agent 33, and they both grinned quickly, then set their mouths into serious lines.

"Excellent answer," Agent 33 said. "You knew that aliens from the planet Wiznut are slower than Earth slugs. An agent could easily run away without getting captured."

Evan felt relieved. Of course he didn't know that Wiznuts were slow—but the agent didn't have to know that.

Agent 564 shook his head. "Our last recruit said he would fight the aliens and take them down. What a dork. Everyone knows that aggressive action against the Wiznuts would lead to interplanetary war."

"We don't need hotheads on this team," Agent 33 said. "Evan, I think you'd make a great agent. Would you like to join us?"

"Sure," Evan said. "But I guess I'd like to know—well, what do you do exactly?"

"We're alien investigators, just like the name says," said Agent 33. "We respond to reports of alien sightings. When dangerous aliens land on Earth, we take steps to keep the planet safe."

That sounded pretty impressive to Evan. "Count me in," he said.

Agent 33 stood up and held out her hand. "Congratulations, Evan."

Evan shook Agent 33's hand, then Agent 564's hand. As Evan and the two agents walked toward the door, the receptionist came in. He held a small white card in his hand. "For the new agent," he said, handing Evan the card. Evan read it:

```
Alien Investigations
Agent 12
```

"Cool," Evan said. "I'm really an agent. Do I get a suit, too?"

"Soon," said Agent 564. "But first you'll need some tools."

Evan followed the agents down the hall. They entered a large room filled with tall, white shelves that reached all the way to the ceiling. Strange-looking tools of all kinds crammed every inch of shelf space.

Agent 564 unclipped the red plastic spy tools from Evan's belt. He left the notebook and the spyglass. "We'll replace your basic stuff," he said. "That alien detector is a fine piece of machinery. How exactly did you come across it?"

Evan told the story of how he had been spying on Sebastian Cream. The agents exchanged knowing looks.

"Yes, we know Sebastian Cream very well," said Agent 33.

"Really?" Evan said. "What's the deal with that guy?"

"That's classified," Agent 33 said. "We don't give rookie agents that kind of information."

Evan felt insulted at first. But, after all, he was a rookie. In fact, he hadn't even planned on becoming an alien investigator. All he'd wanted to do was tell someone about . . .

"Mayor Jones!" Evan cried, suddenly remembering. "He's an alien. I saw him through my spyglass."

Agent 564 nodded. "We know all about Jones," he said. "The mayor is from the planet Blorg. Was he eating onions?"

"He sure was," Evan replied.

"Blorgs love them," Agent 564 said. "I don't understand it, myself."

"So, are the Blorgs here to steal our onions?" Evan asked.

Agent 33 shook her head. "No," she said. "They're here to take over Earth."

Evan felt suddenly nervous.

"We've been onto the Blorgs for some time,"

said Agent 33. "We have several fact-finding missions in the works. We'd like to test you out with one of them. If you succeed, you can become a full-time member of the AI."

"What do I have to do?" Evan asked.

Agent 33 explained the missions. They needed someone small enough to crawl through the air vents in Town Hall and steal a computer chip from the mayor's office. They also needed someone to help them investigate a warehouse on the edge of town. The Blorgs' master spaceship was supposed to be held there.

"But both missions occur at the same time," Agent 33 said. "You need to choose which one you'll go on."

If Evan decides to sneak into the mayor's office, go to page 69.

If Evan decides to investigate the warehouse, go to page 125.

Continued from page 118

Evan had no intention of staying in the basement. When his friend Dave had lived here, they had found a way of getting in and out of the house pretty easily, through the basement window above the washing machine.

Evan climbed onto the washing machine and pushed out the window. It was narrow, but just wide enough to allow him to squeeze through. He tumbled out onto the grass in the Snyggs' backyard.

Evan stood up and brushed the dust from his jeans. He had to tell someone that the Snyggs were really aliens taking over the planet. This was a big deal . . . so he'd have to tell someone big. And there was no one bigger in town than Mayor Jones.

Evan hurried to Bleaktown Town Hall. The old, stone building overlooked Bleaktown Park. Evan jogged there in about ten minutes.

A woman with short black hair and small square glasses sat at the front desk. A sign on the desk read, *Town Clerk*. On the wall behind the desk was a door marked, *Mayor's Office*.

"I need to see the mayor," Evan said, catching his breath. "It's an emergency!"

"What kind of emergency?" the clerk asked.

Evan hesitated. He didn't want to seem crazy. But he had to tell someone. "An alien emergency," he said.

The clerk frowned. "Mayor Jones is very busy right now."

Before Evan could protest, the mayor's door opened. Mayor Jones himself stepped out. He was a tall man with a friendly smile.

"I always have time for Bleaktown citizens," Mayor Jones said. "Come in, young man."

Evan stepped into the office. Mayor Jones sat in a leather chair behind a long, wooden desk. He motioned to a folding chair in front of the desk. "Why don't you sit down and tell me about this emergency?" he asked.

Something about the mayor made Evan feel very comfortable. He launched into the story about the Snyggs, starting with the first time he had seen them through the spyglass.

"And then they locked me in the basement," Evan finished. "I think they're going to take over the world."

Mayor Jones grinned. He stood up. "I'm glad you told me, Evan," he said.

Then the mayor reached up and grabbed the top of his head. He yanked at his thick brown hair. In the next instant, he pulled off his entire face.

Evan gasped. Underneath the human mask, Mayor Jones was an alien!

Go to page 130.

Continued from page 35

"Don't listen to him!" Evan cried. "Mayor Jones is an alien! He's trying to take over the planet!"

Evan rushed to the stage and tugged at the mayor's hair. The crowd gasped. Before the mayor could stop him, Evan pulled off the mayor's human mask.

Shrieks and screams filled the hall. People stumbled over chairs, trying to leave the building. Evan saw the three Snyggs running toward him and the mayor.

Mayor Jones took a small black box from his pocket. "I need transport. Now!" he barked.

Immediately, a bright light flashed on the mayor, catching Evan in its rays, too. Evan covered his eyes. His whole body trembled. When the light dimmed, Evan opened his eyes again.

He and the mayor were not in Town Hall anymore. They seemed to be inside some kind of spacecraft. Blorgs in red uniforms rushed to the mayor. Two Blorgs grabbed Evan by his arms.

"The Earth mission has been aborted," said the mayor. "We must return to Blorg and come up with a new plan."

"What will we do with the human, sir?" one of the Blorgs asked.

Mayor Jones grinned. "Take him to the observatory," he said.

The Blorgs dragged Evan away. He had never been more afraid in his entire life.

At least he didn't order them to destroy me or anything, Evan thought, trying to keep calm. He didn't know what an observatory was, but it didn't sound so bad. Maybe it was a kind of prison. At least it was better than . . . well, Evan didn't want to think about it.

The Blorgs took Evan to a kind of elevator. After a few seconds, the elevator opened up into a long hallway lined with doors. The aliens walked Evan to one of the doors, opened it up, and pushed him inside.

"Feeding time is in three *blarbs*," one guard said.

Feeding time? Blarbs? Evan felt like he was in some kind of nightmare. He looked for a place to sit down and collect his thoughts.

The room wasn't so bad, really, for a prison. There was a soft-looking chair, and a table, and some machines Evan didn't recognize. A huge window took up almost the whole far wall.

Evan sat in the chair and tried to clear his head. The Snyggs would rescue him. In the meantime, he'd have to make the best of things.

Then Evan saw something move outside the

window. He stood up and walked over to the glass.

A group of Blorgs had gathered outside the window. Some were tall and wore red uniforms, but others were small.

Baby Blorgs, Evan guessed.

One of the young Blorgs pointed at Evan.

"Look, Mommy!" Evan heard it say. "A new animal!"

"Don't get too close to the glass," said its mother. "It could be dangerous."

Suddenly, Evan had a horrible feeling he knew what was going on.

He wasn't in Blorg prison. He was on display.

"I'm an animal in an alien zoo!" Evan cried.

THE END

The back wall was closer, Evan figured. He and Simon ran toward it.

Simon reached the fence first and started climbing to the top. He held out his hand to Evan. "Come on," he urged.

Evan reached the fence and stuck one foot into the chain link.

Then the aliens grabbed him.

"Help!" he screamed.

Three aliens held Evan by the arms and began dragging him back toward the building. Evan saw Simon start to climb back down.

"Run, or we'll both get caught!" Evan yelled. "Run and get help!"

Simon hesitated at first, but he realized Evan was right. He jumped over the fence and sped away.

Evan's alien captors climbed back up the wall to the mayor's window, dragging Evan with them. They pushed him through the window.

"What should we do with him, boss?" one of the men asked Mayor Jones.

The mayor motioned toward a door. "In there."

The aliens shoved Evan into a small bathroom and locked the door behind him. Evan sank to the floor, stunned. His mind was racing.

I've been captured by aliens, Evan realized. *What do they want with me?*

There was one way to find out. Evan heard voices through the door. He used the microphone to hear the conversation more clearly.

"Don't worry about the kid," Mayor Jones was saying. "He's one of ours."

"One of ours?" one of the Blorgs asked.

"Of course," the mayor snapped. "Weren't you at the briefing? We hypnotized some of our agents so that they would fit in better with the Earthlings. They think they're humans, not Blorgs. He'll snap out of it in a few hours."

Evan lowered the microphone. He tried to process what he had just heard.

The mayor had said that Evan was one of them. A Blorg. But it couldn't be. He was human! He'd lived in Bleaktown all his life. He was sure of it.

"There's only one way to find out," Evan whispered. He held the spyglass to his eye. Then he faced the mirror.

A hideous alien face stared back at him.

"Oh, no," Evan wailed, panic rising in his chest. "I'm a Blorg!"

THE END

Continued from page 132

Evan didn't know what to think. Aliens surrounded him on all sides. He wasn't sure he could trust any of them.

But at least the mayor was offering him a deal. He couldn't lose with that, right? If the mayor was telling the truth, and the Snyggs were evil, too, he'd be safe.

Evan put the vial on the desk. "Let's make a deal," he said.

"Evan, no!" Simon screamed. "You don't know what you're doing!"

Mayor Jones grinned an evil grin. "See you later," he said, grabbing the vial. Then he ran behind the open panel in the wall. The wall swiftly shut in front of him.

"No!" Mrs. Snygg cried. She hit her alien captor with her elbow. He sank to the ground. Then she picked up her weapon and aimed it at the Blorgs holding Simon and Mr. Snygg.

Zap! Zap! A gold beam of light shot out of the weapon, and those Blorgs disappeared.

The other Blorgs began to screech in high-pitched voices. They shot their weapons at the Snyggs, aiming green laser beams at the family. But the Snyggs expertly dodged each shot.

Evan darted under the desk, terrified. What

was happening? Why were the Snyggs shooting at the Blorgs? And where did the mayor disappear to? Evan began to get a sinking feeling in his stomach.

Finally, the sound of firing weapons stopped. Evan emerged from under the desk and looked around the room.

The Snyggs stood there, their tentacles wiggling on their heads. There were no Blorgs to be seen.

"We got them all!" Simon said happily.

"Not all," Mrs. Snygg said solemnly. "The Blorg leader escaped. We must catch him."

Evan knew they were talking about the mayor. He had made a major mistake!

"So you guys aren't evil aliens trying to take over the planet?" Evan asked, feeling a little silly.

"No," said Mr. Snygg. "We come from the planet Paxus 4. We keep peace in the galaxy. We followed the Blorgs here a few Wiznuts ago. We were coming to capture their leader—until you learned our secret."

Evan felt terrible. "I'm sorry. I didn't know what to do."

"We must hurry," Mrs. Snygg said. "The Blorg leader will not rest until Earth is his. We must find him—if it's not too late."

Mr. and Mrs. Snygg ran out of the room.

Simon turned to Evan and gave him a sad look. "I'm sorry you didn't trust us, Evan," he said.

"Yeah," Evan said. "I'm sorry, too."

THE END

Continued from page 53

"Sure," Evan said. He walked to one of the empty folding chairs and sat down. This had to be his best discovery yet on his spy route. He didn't want to leave until he knew exactly what the UFO Society was up to.

Still, he couldn't bring himself to put on his helmet just yet. He held it in his lap while the gray-haired woman walked over to the circle.

"Welcome, everyone," she said. "I'm Betsy Watson, today's group leader. I'd like to remind everyone to stay for doughnuts and juice after the meeting."

The foil-helmet people nodded and murmured their approval.

"I'd like to begin by taking reports," said Betsy. "Has anyone had an alien encounter this week?"

A middle-aged woman in a jogging suit raised her hand. "I took my helmet off to take a shower, and I could feel the aliens trying to get inside my brain!"

"We're working on an alien-proof shower cap, Lucille," said Betsy. "Anyone else?"

"I saw a guy who looked just like an alien in the Stay 'n' Shop on Saturday," said Alex. "He was buying frozen tacos."

Just about everyone in the circle had a similar

story. While some guy was explaining how his barber was an alien, Alex nudged Evan in the ribs. "Put on your helmet, dude," he said. "The aliens could be picking up everything you're hearing. Totally not cool."

Evan sighed. If he was going to fit in, he'd have to do it. He put the helmet on his head.

Immediately, a weird, sleepy feeling enveloped him. And in the back of his head, he thought he heard a strange, chattering voice.

Evan quickly took off the helmet and stood up. "Sorry, guys," he said. "I'm late for a meeting at the, uh, Bigfoot Society."

Evan hurried to the door and ran to the end of the block. Cautiously, he looked behind him.

A girl his age was coming out of the door of the UFO building. She spotted Evan and started running toward him.

If Evan runs away from the girl, go to page 123.

If Evan waits to see what the girl wants, go to page 41.

Continued from page 122

Evan shook his head. "Sorry, Simon," he said. "There's got to be someone who will believe us. I've got to try."

Simon frowned. "Then you are on your own, Evan Kim," he said.

Evan walked out of the lot and back to Bleaktown Park. The police station was on the way home, but Evan didn't think talking to the police would work. Simon was right. If he strolled in there talking about aliens, they'd think he was joking.

So Evan went straight home, took the phone book out of the kitchen, and brought it up to his room. He plopped the heavy book on his desk and opened it to the government listings.

"There's got to be something in here," Evan muttered as he scanned through the entries. Like the FBI, or something. He looked under "X" for "X-Files," but didn't find a thing. "Rats!" Evan scowled. He sighed and rested his elbow on the desk.

The movement caused the thin pages of the phone book to move, opening to a new section of business listings. Evan leaned over to close the book, when something caught his eye.

Under the heading "Investigations—Private"

was the name of a business: Alien Investigators.

"Alien Investigators?" That sounded just like what he needed. Evan read the ad:

Alien Investigators
The Intergalactic Professionals
We Believe You!
13 Foxwood Lane
Bleaktown

Evan grabbed a pencil and scribbled down the address. This place sounded perfect! There was no phone number, so he'd have to go after school tomorrow.

All night, the hideous alien face of the mayor invaded Evan's dreams. He could barely concentrate in school. When the final bell rang, he raced outside and headed to Foxwood Lane.

13 Foxwood Lane was a narrow, thin, brick building. It looked small, but Evan looked down the slim alleyway on the side and saw that it was actually pretty long.

Evan walked to the front door, adjusted his tool belt, took a deep breath, and pressed the buzzer.

A voice answered him through the intercom: "Come in."

The door made a buzzing sound, and Evan

opened it. He found himself in a lobby that reminded him of his parents' dentists' office. A rectangular fish tank filled with green plants and goldfish sat on a metal stand under the window. A black leather couch faced the receptionist, who sat behind a glass window. He was a serious-looking young man with slicked-back brown hair. He wore a crisp black suit, white shirt, and skinny white tie. He eyed Evan's spy tools as soon as Evan walked in.

The receptionist picked up the telephone. "We've got a new applicant up here," he said in a brisk voice.

"Applicant?" Evan said, confused. "No, I'm here to report an al—"

A door next to the reception desk swung open, and a man and woman stepped out. They both wore identical black suits, white shirts, and skinny white ties. Gadgets and tools dangled from each one's belt. The man had slicked-back blond hair. The woman's short, dark curls were clipped tightly against her head. They looked Evan up and down.

"He looks like a good candidate," the woman said.

The man nodded. "Come on in, sir."

Evan followed them through the door into a small, clean office. The agents sat down in two black chairs and motioned for Evan to sit in a chair facing them.

"I'm Agent 33," said the woman.

"And I'm Agent 564," said the man.

Both agents talked in fast, clipped tones, like the receptionist.

"Uh, hi," Evan said. "I'm Evan."

"So, Evan," said Agent 33, "how long have you been investigating aliens?"

Evan was puzzled. "How did you—I mean, I saw my first alien yesterday, but how did you know?"

Agent 564 pointed to the spyglass on Evan's belt. "That's a classic piece of equipment. A model 218 alien detector. Never fails."

"We're glad you decided to join us," said Agent 33. "Of course, first there's the test. Are you ready?"

The agents were talking so fast that Evan wasn't able to break in and correct them. He found himself getting swept along. These agents wanted him to join them. He liked their suits. And their fancy office. It didn't seem like a bad idea. "Sure," Evan said. "I'm ready."

Agent 564 took a stopwatch from his pocket. He clicked the top button and shouted, "Go!"

Agent 33 started talking super fast. "You are in disguise, infiltrating a meeting of aliens from the

Planet Wiznut. The alien leader shakes your hand, and you offer him your right hand instead of your left. Immediately, he becomes suspicious, because everyone on Wiznut is left-handed. What do you do?"

The hands of the stopwatch ticked on as Evan pondered the answer. This sounded like some kind of trick question.

Maybe, Evan thought, *I should tell them I'd whip off my disguise and take down the aliens. I bet they'd be impressed by that.*

But inside, Evan knew he'd never do that. What he'd probably do is run.

If Evan tries to impress the agents with his answer, go to page 65.

If Evan tells the agents that he would run, go to page 83.

Continued from page 72

Evan didn't want to risk ruining the mission. He quickly climbed back into the air vent and pushed the grate up against the opening. Just then, the office door opened.

Evan froze. Mayor Jones walked into the office with two men in suits. Evan guessed they were Blorgs, too.

The mayor walked to the desk and picked up a cardboard box from the floor nearby. "Sorry, gentlemen," the mayor said. "I forgot my onions. These Earth onions are the best, aren't they?"

The other Blorgs nodded. The mayor handed the box to one of them.

"Lock the door behind me, Axlor," the mayor instructed the other Blorg. "We wouldn't want anyone snooping around here."

The Blorgs left and locked the door behind them. Evan waited until he was certain that they had left. Then he whispered a message to Agent 33. "They're gone," he said. "Can I continue with the mission?"

"Continue," Agent 33 replied. "The building's clear."

Evan swung back down into the office. He opened the top desk drawer. The glass onion sparkled under Evan's flashlight. He grabbed the onion, slipped it into his jacket pocket, and climbed back up into the vent.

Minutes later, Evan was back in the van, handing the onion to Agent 33.

"Well done, Agent 12," said the agent. "Very well done."

Agent 33 dropped Evan back home and told him to be at the AI office by three o'clock the next day. When Evan returned, the receptionist greeted him with a big smile.

"Good work, Agent 12," he said. "Everyone's talking about it."

The receptionist led Evan into the office. Agent 33 and Agent 564 were waiting for him.

"That computer chip held all the information we needed," Agent 33 told Evan. "The Blorgs will not be invading Earth anytime soon."

"That's good," Evan said. "Those Blorgs were pretty creepy."

"You did good work last night, Evan," Agent 33 said. "We'd like you to become a full-fledged member of AI. What do you say?"

Evan couldn't believe it. He was going to be an agent—a real agent. "You bet!" he replied.

THE END

Continued from page 59

Evan and Kelly walked out of the UFO building together.

"So, how does it feel to save the world?" Kelly asked him.

Evan blushed. "Maybe we saved the world this time. But Betsy is right. This isn't over." They reached the end of the street. "I've got something I need to do," he told Kelly. "I'll see you at tomorrow's meeting."

"Sure," Kelly said.

Evan headed toward downtown. He unclipped the spyglass from his belt and held it in his hand.

Without the spyglass, Evan never would have learned about the alien technology inside his helmet. That weird shopkeeper had been right when he'd said it was a special tool. If Mr. Cream hadn't given him the spyglass—well, he didn't know what would have happened. He had a feeling it wouldn't have been good.

Evan walked to Wary Lane and stepped inside the junk shop. Sebastian Cream smiled and stepped out from behind the counter when he saw Evan enter. "So, what did you think about the spyglass?" Mr. Cream asked.

Evan didn't know what twinkling eyes were supposed to look like, but he was pretty sure that's what the little man's eyes were doing. "You were right," Evan said. "It's one-of-a-kind. I'd like to keep it, if that's okay." Evan reached into his pocket and pulled out some folded bills. "I have twelve dollars saved up from my allowance."

Mr. Cream pushed the money away. "No need, my boy," he said. "The spyglass is yours to keep. I think you've earned it." Then he winked.

Evan smiled. "Thanks," he said. "I think I—well, I think it might come in handy again someday."

As Evan walked out the door, he swore he could hear Mr. Cream muttering behind him.

"Sooner than you think, my boy. Sooner than you think."

THE END

Continued from page 82

For the rest of the afternoon, Simon glared at Evan from his desk. Evan sank down in his seat. He felt pretty stupid, calling Simon an alien in front of everyone.

After school, Evan skipped his spy route. He went straight to Sebastian Cream's shop on Wary Lane.

The little man was sitting behind the counter, reading a book, when Evan walked in. He raised an eyebrow when he saw Evan. "Why, hello," he said. "Back so soon? It hasn't been a week yet."

Evan placed the spyglass on the counter. "I've had enough time with this thing. I'm not sure how you rigged the spyglass, but it was very funny. Ha-ha. I guess you got me back for spying on your store."

Mr. Cream closed his book. "Young man, there is nothing funny about this item at all. I do wish you would keep it for a while longer. Perhaps you are giving up too easily."

Mr. Cream sounded deadly serious, but Evan didn't trust him one bit. He had been fooled by the shopkeeper before, and he wasn't going to let it happen again.

"Thanks, but no thanks," Evan said. Then he turned around and walked out.

Back out in the sunshine, Evan felt much better, like a load had been lifted off his shoulders. The sky above was bright blue, shady trees lined the street, and birds sang in their branches. It was a perfectly normal day.

There are no such things as aliens, Evan thought as he walked down the street. *I can't believe I let that guy fool me!*

Then, suddenly, Evan noticed that the birds had gone silent. A dark shadow blotted out the sunshine.

Evan looked up.

A round, silver craft hovered right over the street, just above the treetops.

Evan froze, stunned. It looked just like a flying saucer!

A beam of white light shot out of the craft. Evan tried to run, but the beam paralyzed him. Then, slowly, it began to pull him up into the ship.

I guess there really are such things as aliens, Evan thought.

And then he disappeared into the ship.

THE END

Continued from page 72

Evan decided to take a quick look in the drawer. If he came back without the glass onion, he might fail his mission. He didn't want to take that chance.

Evan opened the drawer. Nothing. He opened another. No paperweight there. His eyes darted around the office, but the paperweight was nowhere in sight.

The voices sounded closer now. Evan had no choice but to give up. He climbed up to the air vent and started to wriggle his way inside.

Just then, the mayor's door opened. Mayor Jones entered, flanked by two men in suits—probably Blorgs. They saw Evan's feet dangling from the vent and rushed to the wall. Evan tried to pull himself inside, but the Blorgs grabbed on to his feet. Evan tried to yank his legs free, but he was no match for the Blorgs. They pulled him out and dragged him in front of the mayor.

"Well, well," the mayor told the Blorgs, "what do we have here? Looks like an AI agent to me."

Evan desperately thought of a way to get out of the mess he was in. "I'm a . . . a janitor," he said halfheartedly. "I was cleaning the vents. They're very dusty."

The Blorgs laughed. They sounded like geese

honking. Then the mayor suddenly stopped, looking angry. "What do you take us for, fools?" he said.

"Let him go!"

Agent 33 burst through the door, holding a weapon that looked like a silver water gun. Evan felt embarrassed and grateful at the same time.

The Blorgs immediately let go of Evan's arms. He quickly ran to Agent 33's side.

"If you pull that trigger, my Blorg army will swarm the building," said Mayor Jones. "You'll never escape."

"Just let us go, and there won't be any trouble," Agent 33 said calmly. "Got it?"

Mayor Jones nodded.

Agent 33 backed out of the doorway, pulling Evan with her. When they were in the hallway, she turned and ran. Evan followed her out of the building and into the van.

"The Blorgs will relocate now," Agent 33 said, her voice tight. "We'll have to start tracing them all over again."

"Does this mean I didn't pass the test?" Evan asked.

"No, you did not pass this test," Agent 33 told him. "In fact, you failed the test miserably! You have ruined our entire mission!"

Evan sighed. If he had just listened to Agent 33, none of this would have happened!

THE END

Continued from page 26

"That's right," Evan said. "My brain is pretty fried from all that geometry Mr. Rieder hit us with this morning."

Evan turned to Simon. Simon just stared at him. "I was just joking," Evan said.

Simon slowly smiled. "Ha-ha. Me, an alien. That is pretty funny."

Evan relaxed. He had half expected Simon to transform into his alien form and blast him with a space ray or something. But Simon was acting pretty cool.

Evan began to wonder if he had been wrong about the whole thing. Sure, the Snyggs looked like aliens through the spyglass. But that could mean that the spyglass was rigged or something. And, sure, he had heard the Snyggs talk about taking over the planet. But they could have been talking about a movie or something. And maybe Simon did have weird clothes, and never went to the bathroom, and ate strange sandwiches. But that could mean that he was different—not from outer space.

For the rest of the day, Evan stopped watching Simon's every move and paid attention to Mr. Rieder instead. When the school bell rang, Simon stepped up to Evan as he started to walk home.

"Would you like to come to my house after school today?" Simon asked.

Evan hesitated. Normally, he would go on his spy route, but he felt pretty bad about having called Simon an alien at lunch. And Simon was being so nice. "Sure," Evan said. "I just need to stop by my house first and let my mom know where I'm going."

Soon, they reached Evan's house. Evan ran inside to tell his mother he was going over to Simon's.

"I will meet you inside," Simon called to Evan. "I need to tell my parents you are coming," Simon said.

Evan knocked on the Snyggs' door a few minutes later. Simon opened the door.

"Come on in, Evan Kim," he said.

Evan stepped into the house and followed Simon into the Snyggs' living room. A white rug covered the floor, blending in with the white walls. The two couches in the room were white, too, although the white cushions rested on silver frames. A silver-and-glass coffee table separated the couches.

Mr. and Mrs. Snygg sat on one of the couches. Mrs. Snygg looked just as she had this morning. Mr. Snygg looked like a taller version of Simon, complete with freckles, except that he wore a black business suit and a blue tie.

"Please, sit down, Evan," Mr. Snygg said, pointing to the other couch.

Evan obeyed. To his surprise, Simon sat on the other couch, with his parents. The three Snyggs stared at Evan, smiling.

At first, no one spoke. Evan fidgeted on the white couch. *This is really weird,* Evan thought. Finally, Mrs. Snygg cleared her throat. "Well, Evan," she said. "Simon told us what happened at school today."

Evan wished he could disappear into the couch cushions. Simon's parents must be pretty mad at him for having called Simon an alien. "I'm really sorry about that," Evan said. "I was just kidding. Honest."

"We do not think you were kidding, Evan Kim," Mr. Snygg said. "We know you are a spy. We know that you have learned our secret."

A creepy feeling swept over Evan's body. The three Snyggs exchanged glances, then nodded to one another. They rose from the couch at the same time.

"You were right, Evan Kim," Simon said. "I am an alien!"

Then the Snyggs' bodies began to flicker like pictures on a movie screen. In the next instant, their human forms evaporated.

Now, three green aliens were standing before

Evan. Tentacles twisted and squirmed out of the tops of their heads. They each had giant gray eyes with no pupils, no noses, and very wide, thin mouths. They seemed to be wearing silver space suits of some kind. Claw-like hands stuck out of the silver sleeves.

"Help!" Evan screamed. He ran for the front door, but a metal panel shot down from the ceiling, blocking his way.

"We will not hurt you, Evan." Evan couldn't tell which alien was talking, exactly, but it sounded like Mrs. Snygg.

The tallest alien—Evan guessed it was Mr. Snygg—spoke next. "Normally, we would not do this. But now that you know our secret, we must keep you safe."

"It will only be for a little while," Mrs. Snygg said.

"What do you mean?" Evan asked. His heart was pounding so loudly, he could hear it in his ears.

The Snyggs surrounded Evan. They picked him up with their claws. Evan struggled, but he couldn't escape.

The aliens carried Evan into the basement.

"Please trust us, Evan," said Simon, the smallest alien. "Stay here until we come back. It's for the best."

And then the aliens left, locking the door behind them.

If Evan tries to escape from the basement, go to page 87.

If Evan trusts Simon and stays where he is, go to page 136.

Continued from page 37

I can always spy on the Universal Fruit Outlet, Evan reasoned, *but this may be my only chance to spy on the mayor.*

The mayor walked up the stairs to Town Hall and entered. Evan took a deep breath and followed the mayor inside the building. Town Hall was a public place, after all.

But there was no sign of Mayor Jones. Instead, Evan found himself facing the town clerk, a woman with short black hair and wire-rimmed glasses. She sat at a desk in the center of the lobby. "May I help you?" she asked.

Evan quickly thought up a lie. "I was, uh, wondering how to get a license for my dog," he said.

The clerk opened up a drawer and began looking through files. Evan used the opportunity to look around. On the wall behind the desk was a door marked, *Mayor's Office.*

Perfect, Evan thought. *It's on the first floor.*

The clerk shoved a piece of paper in front of Evan's face. "Fill this out," she said. "It costs five dollars."

"Thanks," Evan said, backing up toward the door. "I'll bring it back later."

Once outside, Evan ran down the steps to the

empty lot in back of the building. Based on what he had seen, Mayor Jones's office should be right in the center of the building. He took his binoculars off of his belt and scanned the windows.

Bingo! There was Mayor Jones at his desk, and he was opening the box. He reached in and took something out. It looked like . . . an onion?

Evan adjusted his binoculars and looked again. It was definitely an onion, and Mayor Jones was tearing into it like a lion tearing into a piece of steak. He didn't even peel it first. From what Evan could see, the box was full of onions.

"This is definitely weird," Evan muttered. He wished his binoculars were stronger so he could get a better look.

Then he remembered the spyglass. He doubted it would work any better, but it was worth a try. He unclipped it and peered through the lens.

Evan gasped. Mayor Jones didn't look like Mayor Jones anymore. He looked like an alien!

Evan took the spyglass away from his eye. Now the mayor looked normal. Evan looked through the spyglass again.

The mayor definitely looked like an alien. Smooth, gray skin covered his slim body. Two giant white eyes stared out from his face. Weird, wiggly things that looked like squid tentacles extended from the mayor's chin.

Evan lowered the spyglass again and tried not to panic. Crazy thoughts filled his brain. Was the mayor some kind of alien in disguise? Did the spyglass have some kind of special ability to see the mayor's true form? If it was all true—then what was he supposed to do?

"Hello, Evan Kim."

Evan jumped and turned around. Simon Snygg, his new next-door neighbor, was standing there. Simon's red hair was plastered across his head. He was smiling a weird smile.

"Simon? What are you—" Evan began.

"I am spying on the mayor, just like you are," Simon said. "Mayor Jones is not what he seems."

"Then you know!" Evan said excitedly. "You know that the mayor is an alien!"

"Not so loud, Evan Kim," Simon said. "You do not want him to hear you. He can be very dangerous."

Evan lowered his voice. "If he's dangerous, then we need to tell somebody. The police or something."

Simon shook his head. "It is no use, Evan. No one will believe you. It is safer to join with me. We can keep spying on the mayor together."

Simon's offer was sounding suspicious. If the mayor was a dangerous alien, they should tell someone, shouldn't they?

Then again, Simon was probably right. Who would believe them?

If Evan tells someone about the mayor, go to page 100.

If Evan agrees to keep spying with Simon, go to page 15.

Continued from page 99

Evan ran down the street and cut across the nearest backyard, heading toward home. Whatever that girl had to say to him, he wasn't interested. He'd had enough of the UFO Society. And that helmet was just too weird.

Evan suddenly realized that he was still carrying the helmet. Oh, well. He wasn't going to bring it back. Maybe he could trade it to Mr. Cream at the junk shop in exchange for the spyglass. It was a pretty cool tool.

Evan tossed the helmet on the dresser in his bedroom. He did his homework, ate dinner, and played a video game for about an hour before he went to sleep.

Evan was dreaming of silver foil helmets when a strange beeping sound woke him up. He rubbed his eyes and looked around the room.

A thin antenna protruded from the top of the foil helmet. Evan hadn't noticed it before. A tiny red light on top of the antenna was blinking in time with the beeping noise.

"What the—?" Evan reached over to turn on the lamp beside his bed, but suddenly a bright white light filled the room. Evan faced the window, shading his eyes.

A saucer-shaped spacecraft hovered outside his

window! A hatch in the side of the craft opened up to reveal a tiny gray alien with large black eyes.

Evan tried to scream, but no sound came out. He was frozen.

Inside his head, he heard the alien's machine-like voice.

"You Earthlings are so easily fooled," said the alien voice. "We distribute the helmets to the most gullible of your kind. You make the best test subjects. Ha. Ha. Ha."

But I'm not really a member of the UFO Society! Evan screamed inside his head. *I was just visiting!*

But there was nothing he could do. Helpless, he felt a force pull him inside the dark spaceship.

And the hatch snapped shut behind him.

THE END

"It might be cool to see a real alien spaceship," Evan said. "I'll try that one."

Agent 564 nodded. "Meet me here tonight at precisely eight thirty-two," he said. "Bring your tools. And your suit."

"My suit?" Evan asked.

The receptionist walked into the equipment room. He carried a hanger. Draped on the hanger was a black suit, white shirt, and white skinny tie, just Evan's size.

"Wow," Evan said.

Then he thought of something. "How am I supposed to sneak out of my house wearing my agent getup? Won't my parents—"

"Don't worry about your parents," Agent 33 said. "You're an agent now. We'll make sure they understand."

Evan wasn't sure what the agents said to his parents, but he had no trouble leaving the house that night. Agent 564 was waiting outside the office in a black van. Evan hopped in the backseat.

"We've been spying on this warehouse for some time," the agent said. "Suspicious materials have been shipped there. We're pretty sure they're building some kind of spacecraft, but we've never seen it."

He handed Evan a map. "There's an old drainage pipe that leads right to the warehouse floor," she said. "We need you to crawl through it, take some pictures, and then get out. Nothing fancy. Got it?"

Evan nodded. "Got it!"

Go to page 75.

Continued from page 35

"That's right!" Evan yelled, waving his arms. "I'm a spy! An evil alien spy! Look!"

Evan made a goofy face and started dancing around like an idiot.

The crowd laughed. Someone shouted out, "I'm an alien spy, too!"

Mayor Jones's face turned bright red. "Not him, people. It's those people. In the back! I'll prove it!" He pointed to the back row, but the Snyggs were gone.

Evan smiled. At least he had helped the Snyggs escape.

People were getting out of their seats now, muttering to one another and casting strange looks at the mayor.

"Mayor Jones is acting awfully strange," Evan heard someone say.

Soon, Evan was left alone with the mayor, the sleeping Blorgs, and about two men in suits he guessed were Blorgs as well.

The mayor stomped away from the microphone toward Evan. "I will teach you to mess with a Blorg!" he said in a deep, growling voice.

Evan tried to run, but the mayor and the Blorgs had him backed in a corner. The three men ripped off their human faces to reveal their creepy, wide eyes and wriggling tentacles.

"Can't we talk about this?" Evan asked weakly.

The three aliens descended on Evan, their mouths dripping with green saliva. Evan closed his eyes, waiting for the worst.

Thump! Thump! Thump!

Evan opened his eyes. The three aliens had slumped to the floor. Behind them stood the Snygg family.

"Thanks!" Evan said, letting out a relieved breath.

"Thank you, Evan Kim," Simon said. "Your diversion was excellent."

Evan looked around the room at the sleeping Blorgs. "What will you do now?" he asked.

"Paxus 4 is sending a security ship," Mrs. Snygg said. "We will take the Blorgs back to our planet and give them a fair trial."

That sounded good to Evan. He didn't care if he ever saw another Blorg again. But then a sad thought occurred to him. "Does that mean I'll never see you again?" he asked.

"We will only be gone for a short time," Simon said. "But we will return soon, to keep an eye on things. I hope you won't mind having an alien for a friend."

Evan thought about it. Sure, Simon wasn't anything like his old friend Dave. He was really different.

And that was just fine with Evan. "Not at all, Simon Snygg," Evan said. "Not at all."

Go to page 143.

Continued from page 89

Evan stared at Mayor Jones, horrified. He didn't look like the Snyggs at all. His alien face was far more sinister. Two giant white eyes stared out from the slimy gray skin on his face. Sucker-covered tentacles extended from his chin like a wriggling beard.

"You're right about the alien invasion, Evan," Mayor Jones said. His voice sounded like an evil hiss now. "I know, because I'm leading it!"

The mayor walked to the wall and pulled down a wide map of the galaxy. Mayor Jones pointed to a small spot on the map, far away from the picture of planet Earth.

"I come from the planet Blorg," he said. "We have been watching Earth for some time. We will take over your planet, one town at a time. After Bleaktown, all other towns will fall before us!"

Mayor Jones laughed maniacally. He walked back to his desk and pressed a button.

Immediately, the wall behind him slid open. Six more aliens, all exactly like Mayor Jones, stepped out. Instead of wearing business suits, they wore sleek black uniforms. They all carried scary-looking weapons. The aliens surrounded the mayor's desk, making a circle around Evan and the mayor. Mayor Jones leaned over and stared at Evan with all six of his beady eyes.

"The reason I'm telling you all this, Evan," he said, "is because my soldiers will destroy you before you can tell anyone else."

Evan's knees felt like jelly. He looked around for a way to escape, but all he could see were evil aliens at every turn.

Suddenly, the mayor's door burst open. The Snyggs burst in, still in their alien forms. They each carried large, gold-colored weapons. They looked startled when they saw Evan.

"Evan! What are you doing here?" Simon called out.

The Snyggs only dropped their guard for a second, but the evil aliens jumped right in. Three aliens rushed out, and each one grabbed a Snygg.

Evan felt confused. Were the Snyggs from the planet Blorg, too? They didn't look like the evil aliens.

In the next second, Simon Snygg wriggled free from his captor. He pulled a small vial from the belt on his silver spacesuit. "Evan, catch!" he yelled.

Simon tossed the vial across the room, and Evan grabbed it. Mayor Jones stepped back, a look of horror on his hideous face. The other Blorgs stepped away, too. They seemed to be terrified of the vial.

"The stuff in the vial is poison to Blorgs," Simon called out. "Open it up and dump it on him!"

"Don't listen to him, Evan," Mayor Jones hissed. "They're trying to take over your planet, too. Stick with me, and I'll keep you and your family safe during the invasion. You can rule at my side."

"He's lying, Evan!" Simon cried, as another Blorg tackled him. "Use the vial, quick!"

If Evan believes Mayor Jones, go to page 95.

If Evan trusts Simon and uses the vial, go to page 67.

Continued from page 11

As soon as Evan walked through his back door, he smelled his mom's homemade chicken. Suddenly, he felt very hungry.

Evan's parents were dentists who worked in the same office downtown. His mom always got off a little early to come home and cook dinner for Evan and his sister, Tina.

Evan grabbed a banana to tide him over and finished his homework just as his mom called him for supper. He wolfed down his food. Normally, he'd be talking a mile a minute about his day, but tonight he was silent. All he could think about was the spyglass.

After his third helping of food, he made up his mind: He could go out for a little while after dinner with the spyglass, sticking close to home. Just to try it out.

He knew just where to go. A few weeks ago, the Snygg family had moved into the house next door. Evan had always thought there was something strange about them. They had a kid, Simon, who was Evan's age. Simon smiled way too much, Evan thought.

Evan strapped on his equipment belt and headed outside around seven o'clock. He knew the Snyggs' house pretty well, because his best

133

friend, Dave, had lived there before he and his family moved.

Evan crouched down and slowly made his way down his driveway to the clump of bushes on the side of the Snyggs' house. He crept behind the bushes and stepped up onto a large rock at the side of the house.

First Evan used his periscope to peer into the window above, which led into the living room. Perfect! Mr. and Mrs. Snygg and Simon were sitting in chairs, watching television, with their backs to him.

Now to try the spyglass. Evan stood on tiptoe until the top of his head just peeked over the window-sill. Then he unclipped the spyglass from his belt and looked through the lens.

There was the TV . . . and three stuffed chairs . . . but sitting in the chairs were three hideous green monsters!

Evan almost fell off the rock. There had to be something wrong with the spyglass. He looked through the window without it, and saw the Snyggs again, looking quite normal. Then he lifted the spyglass to his eye.

Through the lens, the Snyggs looked just like monsters . . . or more like aliens, maybe. He couldn't see their faces, but the skin on their arms was bright green, and instead of hair, green tentacles squirmed on their heads.

Evan pushed his way out of the bushes, his heart thumping. What he had just seen couldn't be real. It had to be the spyglass. Maybe it was rigged somehow.

He ran out onto the street. Mr. Beemer was out walking his terrier. Evan looked at Mr. Beemer through the spyglass.

He looked normal. So did the dog.

A group of high-schoolers came skateboarding down the street. Evan looked at them through the spyglass.

Normal. They didn't look like aliens at all.

That could only mean one thing: The Snyggs were monsters, or aliens, or worse! He would have to investigate right away.

If Evan decides to sneak into the Snyggs' house, go to page 50.

If Evan decides to question Simon Snygg the next morning, go to page 21.

Calm down, Evan told himself. *The aliens are gone.*

He took a deep breath and looked around the basement as his eyes adjusted to the dim light. There was nothing sinister here, as far as he could see. Just a water heater, a boiler, and a washer and dryer. *This is just a plain old basement, nothing more.*

Evan thought about what to do. Escaping from the basement would be easy enough, if he wanted to. He could run away and tell the world that the Snyggs were aliens.

But something told him not to. The Snyggs had just told him to stay in the basement. They hadn't hurt him. Simon had said to trust him. To his surprise, Evan realized he was willing to do that. "He's not a bad guy, really—for an alien," Evan thought out loud.

So Evan waited. Through a small window above the washing machine, he could see the rays of the sun grow dimmer and dimmer. His stomach rumbled. It was close to dinnertime.

Then he heard the front door open. There were footsteps, and then the basement door opened.

Simon Snygg walked downstairs, wearing his

human form once more.

He was smiling that big, Snygg smile and carrying a large box. "Thank you for waiting, Evan," Simon said. "I am glad you were able to trust me." He set the box on the ground.

"What is going on? Where did you go? What did you do? Who are you?" Evan blurted out the questions.

"My family are spies, just like you," Simon said. "We came to Earth in search of a dangerous criminal from the planet Blorg. He was planning to take over the planet."

So that's what the Snyggs had been talking about, Evan realized. "Did you catch him?" he asked.

Simon nodded. "Yes, we did. And now we are going back home. But first, we have a gift for you." He pointed to the box.

Evan lifted the lid. Inside the box was the largest chunk of gold he had ever seen.

"On our planet, we call this *brak*," Simon explained. "Everything on our planet is made of *brak*. We understand it is very valuable here on Earth."

Evan blinked. "It sure is," he said. "This is worth a fortune."

"It is our gift to you," Simon said. "For trusting us."

"Wow," Evan said, staring at the gold. "It's a good thing I didn't try to escape from the basement!"

THE END

Continued from page 44

It would have been easy to forget all about the helmet and the UFO Society, but Evan just couldn't do it. Something strange was happening—and he wanted to get to the bottom of it.

First, he had to find a way to deactivate the helmet. He couldn't take the chance that it would start messing with his brain again.

Evan tossed the helmet on the bed and ran to the garage. He grabbed a tool kit and raced back to his room. He pulled out a screwdriver and started to work on the helmet. *There must be some way to take this thing apart,* he thought. Finally, he found that, with a little prying, it was easy to get off the first layer of foil—or maybe it was a super-thin metal. He couldn't tell. From there, it was easy to pull out the glowing tubes.

At first, Evan wasn't sure what to do about those tubes. Maybe they were radioactive. He tried to break them in pieces, but they only bent, like some kind of sturdy plastic. To be safe, he buried the tools in the backyard, in a weedy corner where nothing grew.

The next afternoon, Evan went to the UFO Society right after school. Betsy, the gray-haired lady, greeted him warmly. He looked around for Kelly, but couldn't see her.

Evan took a seat in one of the folding chairs, put on his deactivated helmet, and waited.

The meeting started out just like it had the day before. Different people stood up, telling their alien stories. Alex wore the same flying saucer T-shirt he had worn on the day before. Today, he was pretty sure aliens were communicating to him through the fillings in his teeth.

"They, like, tell me to do stuff," Alex said. "Like, to floss after meals."

Evan chuckled to himself. *Those aliens sound like Mom and Dad*, he thought. When your parents were both dentists, you flossed your teeth a lot.

Then, suddenly, Alex stopped talking. His eyes got a dreamy, faraway look in them. Evan watched closely.

"We must build it," Alex said in a strange voice. He sounded like he was in a trance.

Then every member of the UFO Society stood up. They all had the same faraway look that Alex had. *Whoa*, Evan thought. *This is freaky!* "Yes, we must build it," they chanted.

The helmets were making them do it. Evan was sure now. Whatever was affecting the others wasn't doing anything to Evan at all.

"Stop!" Evan yelled, rising to his feet. "Take off your helmets! You're being controlled!"

Every person in the room turned and stared at Evan. He slowly backed up, knocking his folding chair to the side.

"Stop the intruder," Alex said in that spooky voice again.

"Stop the intruder," the others chanted.

Uh-oh, Evan thought. *I think they're talking about me.*

And then, in one swift movement, the UFO Society members converged on Evan, their arms outstretched.

"Take off your helmets!" Evan pleaded. "You don't want to do this!" Evan pushed through the crowd and ran to the door.

Alex was standing there, his arms folded. "Stop the intruder!" Alex cried.

Evan spun around. There had to be another way out.

There was. Betsy Walker stood in front of the door in back of the room, blocking the exit.

"Oh, boy" Evan moaned. He'd have to push his way through, somehow. But should he face Alex, or a sweet gray-haired old lady?

If Evan pushes his way through Betsy's door, go to page 63.

If Evan pushes his way through Alex's door, go to page 77.

Continued from page 129

Saving the planet from the Blorgs felt pretty good—but Evan still had one thing left to do. The next day, after school, he headed straight for Sebastian Cream's Junk Shop.

Evan found Mr. Cream scribbling in a notebook behind the counter in the back of the shop. The little man smiled when he saw Evan enter. "Well, you're back early," he said. "Have you given up on the spyglass so soon?"

"Not exactly," Evan said. "I think I'd like to keep it, if that's okay." If he was going to be Simon's friend, he'd have to be able to help catch aliens. The spyglass seemed like a pretty good tool for that.

Mr. Cream nodded. "Excellent choice," he said.

Evan fumbled in his front jeans pocket. "I have about twelve dollars saved up from my allowance," he said.

"What a coincidence," Mr. Cream replied. "This spyglass costs exactly twelve dollars, tax included."

Evan handed over the money and said goodbye to Mr. Cream. As he stepped back out into the sunlight, he found himself face-to-face with Tania Robbins. Evan and Tania had played on the same soccer team in third grade. Evan had always been a little shy around the tall, pretty girl. He was a little surprised when she recognized him.

"Hey, Evan" she said. "Doing some shopping?"

Evan nodded. "Uh, yeah," he said, suddenly finding himself tongue-tied.

"Me, too," she said. "I'm looking for a present for my grandfather."

Evan wondered what kind of present Tania would find in Sebastian Cream's unusual shop. But he didn't ask about it. He stammered good-bye and headed down the street.

For a second, he thought about hanging around to see what Tania would buy. Maybe he could add her to his spy route . . .

Then he rejected the idea. He had more important things to do now.

Like saving the world.

THE END